I0691375

PACKED COD, HARD ROD

First Edition

Published by The Nazca Plains Corporation
Las Vegas, Nevada
2010

ISBN: 978-1-935509-90-5

Published by

The Nazca Plains Corporation ®
4640 Paradise Rd, Suite 141
Las Vegas NV 89109-8000

PUBLISHER'S NOTE
Packed Cod, Hard Rod is a work of fiction created wholly by *G.W. Leatherman Parks'* imagination. All characters are fictional and any resemblance to any persons living or deceased is purely by accident. No portion of this book reflects any real person or events.

Cover Photo, FleshBlack
Art Director, Blake Stephens

DEDICATION

To jim, a devoted Leatherboy,
who wants both Daddy's flogging
as well as a toaster.

And:

To the Leather Archives and Museum,
for its important work in preserving
our heritage.

PACKED COD, HARD ROD

First Edition

Erotic Literature by the Black Leather Gloved Hands of
G.W. Leatherman PARKS

CONTENTS

ANDREW THE SUIT

I was not initially attracted to the boy seated in front of me. He was, in my mind, effeminate and self-important. Yet something intrigued me about him and I considered it a challenge to dominate him sexually.

He was in charge of an agency that had leverage over a contract which I wanted for my company. With his slicked-back hair, polished fingernails, French cuff shirt with gaudy gold cufflinks, and overabundance of cologne, he presented an arrogant self-assurance and little respect for the man who sat in front of him. Little did he know that he was seated in front of a man whose heart normally beat under a layer of black Leather and enjoyed the pleasures of beating prissy little assholes into submission. For the interview I had suppressed my Leatherhood with a respectable pair of jeans (the ass wasn't torn out) and I had even put on a tie.

The interview did not go well as he continually talked to me as if I was an uneducated moron.

I held my temper because I really wanted the contract. Revenge would come later.

By the end of the interview, he had warmed up a little. I treated him with respect, responding softly, but firmly, as I did to all my boys, showing him more respect than the little prick deserved.

We concluded our meeting, the first of several, by shaking hands. I noticed that he flinched as I gripped his hand a little too strongly. Maybe he was afraid he would break a nail.

Our next two meetings were more successful and by the end of the third, he was even a bit flirtatious. By the fifth meeting, I had secured the contract with his promise that he would help in any way he could. We were now on a first-name basis. I occasionally rubbed my crotch which seemed to temporarily distract him each time.

With the announcement of the award of the contract, I held a small party at my house to celebrate. I invited the boy even though I did not think he would condescend to show his prissy little ass, but I was wrong. He showed up, reeking of cologne and sporting a three piece suit. He seemed to take in every detail – the Leather furniture, the collection of homoerotic drawings and other artwork, scattered discretely throughout. He showed no reaction.

He balanced uneasily on the arm of my Leather sofa and began talking to Brittany, my attractive assistant-blonde, good-looking. *"If you are trying to make time with her, pal, you're wasting your time. She's a dedicated lesbian,"* I thought, *"Her partner is a purebred dyke who could whip your pussy ass with one hand tied behind her back…"*

He remained on the arm of the sofa for some time and downed several stiff drinks before accidentally slipping off the arm of the sofa. His composure broken, he moved to the edge of the room and remained there for some time.

I finally went over to him and offered a tour of the rest of the house. He made few comments as he viewed my weight room, the walnut-paneled library with a walk-in humidor, and the bedroom outfitted with a Leather bedspread and pillows. Little did he know that the closet led to a secret dungeon outfitted with a sling, manacles, and other S&M pleasure items.

"Do you mind if I sit down for a few moments?" he asked, *"I really don't feel well."* I sat him down in my black Leather chair and returned to the party downstairs.

An hour later the party broke up and I had quite forgotten about the boy in my bedroom. I saw my last guests to their cars and locked the backdoor before retreating upstairs.

I climbed the steps and went immediately to my dressing room where I ripped off the white collar shitwear that I wore for the party and put on my favorite chaps, boots and a pair of tight, black gloves. My cock and balls hung down my Leathered leg as I then went to the humidor and selected a heady cigar. As I entered the bedroom, I noted the boy asleep in my chair.

I stood between his spread legs and slowly untied his tie, unbuttoned his vest and pink shirt. His chest was handsome with a line of fur extending down into his pleated trousers. *"Too much to resist,"* I mused, as I unbuttoned the trousers. A handsome cock and balls were housed in a pair of, what else... silk shorts. I leaned over and rubbed his cock with my gloved hands. His cock quickly responded to the Leather gloves, but he still remained sleeping. I pulled his head toward my cock and placed it squarely in his mouth. *"This will wake you up, boy."*

"What...?" he sputtered as my cock in his throat woke him. He attempted to get out of the chair, but I pushed him back into place.

"You're in the Leatherman's lair, now, boy..." As I crawled on top of him, holding him in place with my muscled arms.

He protested and so, I grabbed a black bandana from the nearby nightstand and shoved it in his mouth.

He continued to struggle. *"Relax, boy... you're in Daddy's control and you will be until I finish with you. Make it easy on yourself and submit to me..."*

He shook his head violently. He mumbled and sputtered while continuing to shake his head. His coiffed hair fell over his eyes, giving him the boyish quality I wanted to see.

I rubbed my Leathered hands over his face. I leaned toward him and engaged his mouth in a forceful kiss. He continued to protest. His hands reached up and was beating me on the back. Shit, I thought, I should have handcuffed him to the chair.

I continued to kiss him as he continued to struggle. Just made the conquest more challenging.

I flattened my Leathered body against his. His cock arched upward and I could feel it pulsing against my cock. *"Damn,"* I thought, *"I wish I had my cod with the metallic spikes on it which would be pressing into his shaft."*

I continued to explore his mouth and my hands were now pulling on his handsome nips. They were large ones and I took great pleasure in pulling on them as he continued to flail my back.

He continued mumbling.

I finally reached my saturation point and slapped him hard against his left cheek. He stopped as tears welled up in his eyes.

"Shut the fuck up, bitch." I sternly warned him, *"or else your punishment will be even more prolonged."*

I guess maybe he finally rationalized that I meant business and he stopped struggling…at least, for the moment.

"That's better, son. Now, stand up." He was unsteady on his feet as he rose from the chair. He lost his balance and fell into my waiting arms.

"Come with me…" as I placed my hands firmly around his neck. He was apparently still woozy from the alcohol he had consumed as I lead him to my dungeon/playroom.

Before he could protest, I secured his wrists to restraints and his ankles to similar restraints. The boy was now positioned on my St. Andrew's cross. I quickly hooded him and placed a buttplug in his mouth. He had no chance to scream as I maneuvered the plug in while removing the bandana. His chest was heaving. I quickly added a blindfold.

I pulled the silk shorts down around his ankles and viewed a really handsome cock. Despite his protests, it was saluting me.

I massaged it with my gloved hand while the other hand explored his handsome ass. He really was very athletic.

I thought at this point that there was still hope that I could turn him into a man's boy.

I worked on that boy for close to two hours, alternately flogging and paddling him and talking to him, relaxing him, trying to calm him down. He still shook his head violently at times, but you could see I was wearing the boy down.

"Relax, boy. Everyone is gone – just you and your Leathermaster…." With that I removed the plug from his mouth.

"Let me out of here, you fucking pervert… I'm not interested."

"Yeah, I can see from your throbbing cock that you aren't interested, boy."

He continued to protest, so I shoved the plug back in his mouth and continued the assault on his well-tuned body.

By and by, he was struggling less and stood silently as I continued the assault.

A half hour later, I once again pulled the plug out of his mouth. He whispered, *"Thank you, Sir."*

"That's better, son." He nodded, with his eyes downcast.

I reached down and pulled his jaw toward mine. I thrust my tongue in his mouth. And this time, he responded. His tongue began to explore my mouth.

The boy's spirit had been broken and I knew that the process to Leather boyhood could finally begin. I unshackled him. He stood in place with his head lowered.

I stripped him of the silk shorts and tore them into several pieces – they would service me well as cum rags.

I escorted him to the shower where I washed away the offensive cologne. All the time, he said nothing.

I toweled him off and escorted him to the bed where I lay on top of him, massaging his wrists, rubbing his nips and ribcage, pressing my dick against his. His dick responded and soon, he asked permission to cum.

I denied the request and threatened him with a further flogging. His face grimaced as he tried to control his cock, but within minutes, he shot a load.

I dismounted him, retrieved one of my new cum rags and smeared his cum all over his face and chest.

"Back to the dungeon, boy."

He was flogged for disobeying his new Master. He would learn. He would earn his disciplinary bad 'marks', but he would learn.

You should see my boy now. He no longer wears the French cuff shirts and cologne. He greets me at the end of the day in Leather jock (a present from his Leatherman) and boots. He is a true Leatherboy, making his Leathermaster prouder of him each day. Only a few months before, I'm sure he would have found it repulsive to lick a man's dirty Leather boots or to take ash from his Leatherman's cigar, but now he relishes it. It 'suits' him.

A SESSION, MULTIPLIED BY TWO

The two most beautiful things in the world to me are: 1.) a Leatherman in full, black Leather marching proudly down the street – shined boots, crotch-tight pants with an attached cod, motorcycle jacket, Damascus gloves, and a Muir cap. It turns my crank every time. 2.) the sight of a boy's naked ass presenting itself to me for my use.

I had agreed to meet a boy in Philadelphia on the weekend I'm about to describe. I wasn't sure what to expect. We had met on the internet and chatted a number of times. This led to telephone conversations of raunchy S&M talk and eventually to the appointment at hand.

I'm not one to pack my Leathers and hide behind a pair of jeans and a tee shirt. I journey in full Leather and don't really give a fuck what other people think. At the rest stop, you are cruised more than once by straights who quickly avert their eyes and strike up a conversation with their nearby wife. But you see out of the corner of your eye, that second look. Wonder how many cocks have hardened as the result?

I made the journey in two hours, stroking my cock occasionally, pulling on the chain connecting my nip clamps to my aching tits. An aromatic cigar clenched between my teeth. I had taken my car because I had brought a large bag of toys and a change of Leather for the sessions ahead.

The boy's emailed instructions had been very clear and I found his house in a respectable neighborhood of the downtown area. Again, I wasn't sure what to expect but was pleasantly surprised to see that it was a tree-lined street with pots of flowers out on the steps. And lots of parking!

I parked a block or so away from the address and unloaded my equipment. Several people walked by as I unloaded. I'm sure that I was the topic of conversation as they continued to their destination.

As I mounted the steps, there was a discrete note on the door. *"Sir,"* it read, *"the door is open. I am ready to serve you, I'm on the second floor."* I marched confidently in, viewing a tastefully decorated interior, with lots of artwork on the walls.

"Boy, your Leathermaster is here," I yelled, so as not to surprise the boy too much.

I heard only a gurgled response and so, I marched up the staircase.

I found the boy in the second bedroom. He had manacled his feet to the two corners of the bed and was lying facedown with a beautiful muscled ass slightly raised. He was a smooth-skinned boy. Nice definition of shoulder and arm muscles. He held on to the other bedposts. He had hooded himself.

"Afternoon, boy." as I slapped his ass with my gloved hand.

The boy's response was a slight dipping of his head into the pillow.

I unpacked my equipment on a nearby chair, first pulling out a pair of wrist restraints. They were tied into place with pieces of bondage rope.

I slapped his ass again. His ass was firm and his back arched slightly as I administered several more slaps. I unpacked my selection of floggers and paddles.

I began rubbing his ass with my gloved hands, squeezing and pulling. Spreading the asscheeks and exploring with two fingers. Hell, this was going to be fun.

I leaned down and briefed him on my projected rotation of floggings and he simply shook his head. I could see that he had inserted a plug in his mouth, it snapped to the hood.

"Let's get to work, boy."

I administered, in quick succession, a test with the five floggers I had brought. Twenty lashes from Numbers #1-#5 – mild floggings from each. Number #4 elicited the most provocative response – a groan and a more pronounced arching of the back. He had chosen his own item of torture. I placed that in my memory bank.

I brought out my three butt paddles. I intensified the paddlings and the boy moaned as Number #3 'hit home'. I registered that in my memory bank as well.

We went through a second rotation of both – just to make sure that my test results were accurate. They were.

The boy began to flinch as the floggers and paddles left a matrix of marks on his asscheeks. His back soon had similarly markings.

As my horniness set in and my male pouch expanded with my excited cock, I increased the number of times I struck.

The boy began moaning and occasionally vocalizing the pain he felt.

My cock began to pulse within its Leather confines.

I would occasionally slap the reddened areas with my gloved hand, but really enjoyed hearing the whack of the floggers and paddles.

That beautiful ass was now covered with a mesh of red marks as I brought down Flogger #4 as fucking hard as I could. The boy's body jolted.

"Lie still, boy!" I commanded, *"that was just one lash. There are twenty-nine to follow."*

And I administered those in quick succession. The boy's body was wrenching from side to side as the raw Leather hit his raw ass.

A protracted scream from the boy's mouth was heard after the fifth strike and continued well into the twentieth. He was silent after that.

The butt paddle added to his misery. Thirty strong paddlings and the boy was screaming again. He settled down after the fifteenth or so.

All the while, my cock was throbbing. It wanted a piece of the action. I knelt in between the boy's legs and spitting on my cock after extracting it from its cod, I inserted it slowly up the boy's fuckhole. He screamed again as I thrust it in and out of his ass.

I reached up and roughly pulled his hooded head toward me.

"Take it, boy, take your man's cock… you know you want it!"

The only response I got was a groan. So be it. This was about pleasuring me.

I rode that boy's ass for only a short time before my cock released a gob of jism into the inner recesses of the boy's ass.

Crawling off the boy, I picked up the butt paddle and gave him twenty more paddlings. My cock was dripping cum. I roughly pulled his head up and removed the buttplug from his mouth. Wiping the cum with my gloved hand, I made him lick it off my gloved fingers.

Taking off the restraints, I rolled the boy over in his bed. His cock was throbbing. I milked it with my gloved hands, warning him not to shoot. Despite his Master's warning, he shot a load all over his belly.

I slapped him roughly on the cheek. Spying a pair of underpants discarded on the floor, I wiped up the cum from his belly. He would not taste his own cum. I tied his wrists to the bedposts.

For disobeying his Sir by shooting before allowed, he would receive a similar barrage of floggings on his chest. I made sure that the tails connected with his rib cage, his nips, and his shoulders. The boy's head rolled from side to side.

Damn, I was enjoying this. He was a good subject for this Leatherdaddy's sadistic tendencies.

I undid the ropes and rolled him on his belly. Using the rings on the ankle restraints and the wrist restraints, I now tied his arms and legs together with a length of bondage rope. He made a neatly wrapped package, his hands touching his feet. Red marks visible on most of his floggable surfaces.

He remained silent and motionless as I climbed onto the bed. I sat at the head of the bed with my booted feet tightly surrounding his body. I rested his hooded head on my cod.

My cock, enjoying the pressure of the boy's head, reacted by stiffening. I had not gagged his mouth and so, I unsnapped my cod. My cock arched into his mouth. The boy had no alternative but to swallow as much of it as he could.

He began sucking greedily as I pulled my cock in and out of his mouth.

As he continued to suck, his body raised and lowered, going down on my manrod. With his hands and feet bound together, I was impressed by the control the boy was able to achieve. And I was going to take advantage of this 'talent'.

I grabbed the back of his head and pushed it down on my swollen cock.

He choked momentarily, but recovered and continued his duties.

"Good boy," I remarked, as I forced his head down to the shaft of my cock.

Since I had cum just a few minutes before, it was some time before I could 'reload' and shoot. I didn't mind the interlude. I relaxed, stroking his hooded head, pushing it down when I thought he wasn't swallowing the whole cock. He was a good boy, knowing that he was born to serve a LeatherMaster like me.

As I was nearing climax, I held a steady pressure on his head, pushing his head down on the shaft on my cock. It throbbed with anticipation of shooting a load as the boy sucked harder and harder.

Just then, I heard the front door open and close. A man's voice yelled, "Son, your Master is here…"

"What the fuck?" I demanded.

The boy pulled back and struggled in his restraints.

I jumped off the bed and strode to the staircase.

A man, outfitted in heavy black Leather, was coming up the stairs.

"What the fuck?" he said, as he saw me.

He came into the bedroom. "Who the hell are you?" he demanded of me.

"I'm asking the same fucking question… You interrupted my session with this boy." My cock was still fully erect, and dripping precum.

"I have an appointment with this boy at 4 o'clock."

"I had an appointment with this boy at 2:30."

We both agreed that the boy had some explaining to do as I slapped the side of his hooded head with a hard slap from my gloved hand.

He stammered to get an answer out but not giving us a satisfactory answer, fell silent.

I ushered the other Leatherman (whose name was Jack) out in the hallway for a conference. We agreed that we would work over this bad boy.

Jack had a similar set of floggers and paddles.

For the next two hours, that boy got the beating he deserved. I was on the left. Jack was on the right.

We took off the ropes which hogtied the boy into place. The boy was once again tightly manacled to the bedposts.

His ass got fisted not once, but twice.

He swallowed a lot of cum from both of our over-excited cocks.

Instead of one hundred lashes, he got two hundred.

In this protracted session, the boy screamed as the lashings intensified. His body must have been on fire because his ass was glowing red by the time we finished that rotation. We left him manacled to the four corners of the bed. For good measure, I jammed the gag in his mouth and a buttplug up his ass as Jack and I went downstairs and poured ourselves drinks from the boy's well-stocked bar. We lighted cigars and quickly became friends, brothers under the black skins.

"I think, Buddy, we should go to the bar for awhile and let the boy reflect on his transgressions," Jack suggested.

"I was just thinking the same thing. But you know, how did that little fucker know how long I wanted to abuse him? Too presumptuous on his part – – to arrange for another man to beat his ass." The thought made my anger instantly boil over and I started up the stairs, ready to redden his ass even more, but Jack caught me by the crotch and drew me toward him. We kissed, thrusting each other's tongues into one another's mouths. Our Leathers collided and we were soon rolling around on the floor, tearing at each other's codpieces. We 69'd on the floor until we had exhausted one another's manhoods.

Repairing ourselves, we headed out to the bar, leaving the bound boy to reflect on booking two Leathermen for one afternoon. He had no other choice. He was under our control.

Two proud Leathermen marched down the street and to the Leather bar, only a few blocks away.

We must have cut quite a figure, two men in full black Leather, our cods bulging, our spit-shined boots clicking against the pavement. We formulated a plan for the rest of the evening and after a couple of hours and a couple of beers, returned to our makeshift dungeon.

The session continued until the wee hours of the morning. A session, multiplied by two, that the boy would never forget.

FOOTBALL SUB

My Leatherdaddy was stretched out in his Leather easy chair – his booted feet propped up on the ottoman. He absently stroked his cod as I prepared his cigar for him. I clipped it carefully so there were no ragged edges. I knelt before him with bowed head and presented his cigar to him. He took it from my outstretched hands and placed it in his mouth. I struck the match on the side of the matchbox, sheltering the flame with the palm of my hand and held it toward the end of the cigar. It lighted on the first try. His black Leather gloved hand conveyed it to his mouth and he drew on it deeply. His head arched backward as the second, long draw completed the fire circle at the end. He blew a smoke ring toward the ceiling. It was then that he reached down and patted my hooded head.

"Good boy," he said.

"Thank you, Sir." I replied.

I knelt beside his chair as his gloved hand caressed my hooded head.

My eyes were momentarily distracted by the outline of his cock in his codpiece. I looked back at his face.

His eyes were closed as he continued to stoke the cigar. It was my Master's first cigar of the evening and he deserved it, after a long day at work.

He continued to absently rub my head. With his other hand, he fondled his crotch. The cigar was firmly clenched between his teeth.

He motioned me to crawl closer. I responded like a willing puppy.

He motioned for me to kneel beside the chair, near the right arm, facing in the same direction as he was.

With that, he placed his arm around my neck and covered my nostrils with his Leather gloved hand. The combined smell of Leather and cigar smoke on the glove was the most erotic smell. Well, second to the smell of my Master's warmed cock in his Leather cod.

My Daddy massaged my face with that gloved hand. "Fuck!" I thought, "my cock is already hardening. The smell of my Master's Leather and smoke is enough to make me cream." Daddy knew what he was doing. He continued to fondle his enlarged cod while he continued to massage my face with his glove.

He puffed on the cigar, drawing deeply at times, releasing plumes of hazy smoke into the air. The cigar was so fucking aromatic. My cock continued to harden.

As the ash lengthened, my Master motioned for me to kneel between his legs. He leaned forward and trapping a burst of smoke in his mouth, he pulled my jaw toward his. My mouth was fully opened as he blew the smoke into my mouth. He had trained me to receive his smoke. I trapped it within my own mouth, and then slowly released it.

"Good boy," Daddy said. He did it several more times. Each time, the smoke tasted so good as I trapped it and released it to Daddy's satisfaction.

All the time, I kept a watchful eye on Daddy's cod. It was now tented; the muscular head of his cock could be seen straining against the Leather. Tonight, my Master had chosen to wear his black Leather uniform. It was accented with white piping. He wore matching wrist gauntlets. His spitshined Dehners. He looked like every boy's cop fantasy. Only this was real life. I was his boy. He was my LeatherMaster.

"Are you ready to taste another kind of cigar, boy?" Daddy asked.

I shook my head and replied, "Yes, Sir."

"You know what to do, boy, you have my permission." I slowly unsnapped the cod. His beautiful cock was released. I worshipped that cock.

I began a very slow tongue massage of the head, wrapping my tongue around that beautiful specimen of manhood. I trailed my tongue down the throbbing shaft. His handsome balls were not to be missed, as I lifted each one with my tongue and licked them.

I repeated the procedure over and over again. I hoped he would not cum for some time. I so enjoyed this activity. His cock began throbbing, the veins prominently viewed along the shaft. The cockhead became even more swollen. A drop of dew appeared in the piss slit. I flicked my tongue in and out, catching the precum. My Master's cum was something of which I relished every drop.

My Leatherdaddy continued to smoke his cigar. The aroma of the cigar was surrounding me. I briefly glanced up to view my Daddy massaging his nipples through his tight Leather shirt. I wanted to suck on those too.

I continued sucking his handsome rod. It pulsed in my mouth. I felt the head on the roof of my mouth. I caressed the shaft with my lips as I took more and more of the entire cock in my mouth. Daddy began moaning softly. He began pumping his cock in my mouth. He sucked harder and harder on the cigar as I began a more vigorous sucking.

My Master exploded in my mouth with his delicious gift of cum. I savored the taste. I continued to tongue the cock until it had returned to its normal state.

"Thank you, boy. Good work," he patted me on the head. I smiled. I thought, "Anything to please my Master."

I knelt obediently beside him until receiving his next order.

"Boy, my ash is lengthening. Open your mouth."

I opened my mouth and stretched out my tongue. He dropped a delicious long ash on my tongue. It tasted so good as I chewed on it slowly, the ash dissolving in my slavemouth.

"Thank you, Sir."

We repeated the smoke inhalation several more times. My Leatherman relaxed in his chair, pulling absently on his recovering cock.

When his cock had recovered to full length, I asked, "May I taste your cock once more, Sir?"

He granted me permission and I took the throbbing rod within my mouth once more. Fuck, it tasted so good.

I relaxed the back of my mouth and took the whole shaft right down to the balls.

My Master was leaning back in his chair, moaning softly. I knew my tonguing was doing the job it was meant to do.

"Turn around, boy."

I knew what that meant. I released his cock from my mouth and began slowly squatting, until his dick was inching up my hole.

My Leatherman began a slow pumping, inching his cock until it was fully inserted into my fuckhole.

Daddy unsnapped his Leather shirt and began twisting on his aroused nipples. He continued to pump slowly up my ass. He apparently increased the intensity on his nips because he was moaning more loudly. His cock rose and fell within my butt cavity.

It felt so delicious.

As Daddy continued to pull on his nips, he increased the pumping action. I began sliding my ass up and down, moving in concert with his rhythm.

With a final thrust, Daddy came up my ass. The cum dribbled out onto his Leathered legs.

I continued to take his cock until he ordered me to lick it clean.

I tongued the cock clean and then licked the cum off his Leathers.

Daddy sat motionless as I was performing this duty.

"Boy," Daddy said, "it's time for kick off."

"Yes, Sir," I replied.

I turned on the television just as the kick off was seen. The Steelers had the ball in their possession. They marched down the field quickly, with one beautiful spiraled pass after another. Daddy was fully engaged in watching the game, but still had time to fondle my hooded head and massage his inactive cock.

My attention was on Daddy's cock which hardened as he watched the game. The quarterback reared back to throw into the end zone and was sacked.

"Fuck!" Daddy yelled. "Down on the floor, boy."

I obeyed and Daddy proceeded to flog my back and ass fifteen times for the fuck-up of the football team.

Daddy was agitated as the opposing team took possession of the ball. He was muttering and cursing. He puffed more vigorously on his cigar. His cigar was half-smoked when he said, "Boy, bring me another cigar and my cigar tube."

That could only mean one thing as I obeyed his orders. He inserted the cigar in the tube and instructed me to bend over. He inserted the tube in my asshole and ordered me to warm it up until he was ready for it.

The opposing team was advancing down the field and Daddy was not a happy man. After a series of successful first downs, the team walked into the end zone. They scored the extra point.

"Fuck!" Daddy yelled again. I dropped to the floor at his instruction and received twenty more lashes of his flogger on my back and ass.

In the second quarter, the Steelers rallied and scored two touchdowns. Daddy rubbed my head and said, "Good boy!" as if I had had something to do with their success. I was grateful for the respite from flogging.

At half-time, the Steelers were ahead 14-7.

"Get me a beer, son," Daddy ordered. I quickly retrieved it and he took a long swallow from it. "I'm ready for my cigar, son." I extracted the cigar from my warming hole, removed it from the cigar tube, clipped it, and presented it on bended knee to him. As he held it to his lips, I struck a wooden match and made sure that it was evenly lighted before extinguishing the match.

The third quarter saw the Steelers rally. Defense intercepted a throw and pretty soon, they added another seven points to their score.

The opposing team fought back with a vengeance, however, as they quickly maneuvered down the field on the very next play. "What the fuck?" Daddy yelled as the defense seemed to open up and let the player gain thirty yards. Daddy was mad again.

First and goal and Daddy pulled his butt paddle off his belt. I knew what to expect unless a miracle occurred. But it didn't and the fuckers scored another touchdown and the extra point. Daddy got out of his chair, lined me up against the mantle and struck my ass thirty times. It hurt like hell. He was pissed.

Steelers ball and they did absolutely nothing with it. Daddy's eyes were riveted to the television screen as the fuckers once again took possession.

The quarterback threw an incredible pass down the field. "Miss it. Miss it," I silently pleaded with his intended receiver. He caught it as if he was caressing a baby.

Daddy once again leapt out of his chair and paddled my ass a total of forty times. He was cursing the whole time.

Needless to say, within minutes, the opposing team had scored another seven points, tying the game.

The fourth quarter was dismal. The Steelers' confidence seemed to have disappeared and they made a bunch of stupid mistakes, resulting in loss of yardage through penalties.

I looked at Daddy's face. He was furious. He began pacing in front of the television – cursing at the Steelers. Cursing at their opponents. I knew who would pay if they lost. Or more to the point, whose ass would pay.

At the two minute warning, the score was tied.

The opposing team had possession. They played the game carefully and with only a few seconds left, advanced with a field goal, 24-21.

"Damn!" Daddy yelled. He looked at me and ordered me down to the dungeon.

He quickly manacled me to the St. Andrew's Cross. My ass, back and shoulders were flogged more times than I can remember. In his defense, Daddy had to take out his frustration on someone and I was his willing boy. After the seemingly endless rotations of floggings, Daddy had calmed down.

With that, the Leatherman began rubbing his cock, which was recuperating in its Leather cod. He leaned against a supporting post while I remained facing the wall, I could only guess that his cock was becoming excited.

Daddy pulled his cock out of the cod and began massaging it into fullness. The man was caressing it, lubricating it with the spit on his gloved hand.

Like a well-greased dildo, he eased it up my willing ass. He reached around and was pulling hard on my sensitive nips. His pinch was intense and I moaned as it excited my dick. He reached down, pulled on my cock, and gripped my balls with great intensity. I moaned even more.

Daddy began pumping his cock in and out of my shaft.

He pushed his cigar into the mouthhole of the hood and I was forced to puff vigorously on his cigar.

It excited me even more as Daddy continued to push his cock in and out of my fuckhole.

"Fucking Steelers. Damn them. They fucking gave away that game. Next week, they better improve their game. I'd like to have one of their asses. I'd plow it. I'd fucking plow it."

He had worked himself into a frenzy and came in my ass. Jism squirted out on the floor.

He withdrew his cock and stepped away.

He took the manacles off my wrists and ankles and turned me around. He drew deeply on his cigar and cupping my mouth, blew smoke into my eager mouth. I released it slowly to his satisfaction. At his command, I then licked his cock clean.

"Now, get down on the floor and lick up my spilled cum."

I licked it up willingly, mixing it with the grit and dirt of the floor.

"Good boy. You're a good cigar boy."

As he rubbed my aching back and ass, he quietly said, "They play again next week, son. Be here for kick off."

"I'll be here, Master," I thought, "I just hope they lose again."

CONFESSION IS GOOD
FOR THE SOUL

The handsome submissive stood facing the garage wall. His hands were tied to a sturdy pipe, stretching above his hooded head. He was naked. He shivered as the temperature in the garage responded to the setting sun. The Master told his boy that he would return soon for a spirited flogging session. At this point, the boy would have welcomed the heat of his Master's body and the heat of the Leather straps as they made contact with his naked flesh. All the boy could do was wait.

The LeatherMaster disappeared out the garage door. The boy heard the click of the lock as the garage door was locked from the outside. He heard the crank of his LeatherMaster's cycle and the cycle opening up as the Leatherman disappeared down and out of the driveway. There was no chance of escape or of rubbing his body with his arms and legs. Both arms and legs were manacled with restraints and then tied into place with sturdy bondage rope.

The boy could only stand silently. His mind wandered to various topics, just to keep himself as alert as possible. His hearing was muffled by the black Leather hood. His eyes were covered with a snapped-on blindfold. The LeatherMaster had also inserted two plugs – one in the boy's mouth and one up his ass. The LeatherMaster told the boy to hold the plug in his ass – he would have more hell to pay if it eased out.

As he thought more and more, the boy began to dread his LeatherMaster's return. He had been a bad boy and had not immediately confessed his transgressions to his LeatherMaster. "Well, actually…," the boy rationalized, "he really didn't give me any time to talk before he hooded me and plugged me…"

"Still," the boy's thoughts continued, "I should have begged to speak to him before he placed me in bondage."

His LeatherMaster had allowed him freedom for a weekend – a test, and he had fucked up.

The boy had responded to an internet connection and traveled to be a boyslave for the weekend. The guy was handsome, Leathered, but totally inexperienced in S&M. His flogging was sloppy and didn't hurt. He clumsily placed the boy in bondage rope on top of a workover table. The ropes were so loose that the boy could have walked away. As it was, the novice sadist finally extricated the boy from the ropes and requested that the boy suck him off.

"Now, if that had been my Sir," the boy concluded, "he would have pushed me down on my knees and stuck his cock in my face…"

But, as ordered, the boy sucked the man's cock which ejaculated only minutes later.

That apparently was all the guy wanted and the boy left, not aroused, not even feeling vaguely satisfied. The would-be sadist just wanted a blow job.

That action would have been fine, but the boy wanted more.

He remembered seeing a bar about twenty minutes away from his initial destination – the bar looked sleazy. The boy hoped so, he needed to be worked over by a Leatherman.

Although he couldn't remember the name of the bar, its logo was the head of a man wearing a Muir cap and sporting a handlebar mustache.

The boy parked his car and went inside.

The hour was early and so there were only a few barflies nursing their bottles of beer.

The boy ordered a water and cruised the entire contents of the bar. "Pretty dismal," he thought.

He stood in the darkened corner of the bar, nursing his water and absently rubbing his crotch.

The usual crowd filtered in. One or two guys in Leather came in, but they were probably bottoms. They wore bar vests and tee shirts.

He ordered a second water and returned to the same corner. As he turned around to prop his foot against the wall, a big bear of a man entered the bar. He was in full Leather, dripping with chains and a flogger attached to the D ring of his pants.

You could tell he was a 'take-charge' kind of guy. Oddly enough, he was by himself.

As the guy paid for his beer, he cruised the bar. His eyes rested on the boy momentarily before continuing his sweep of available boys.

The boy was surprised when the Leatherman sauntered over to him and placed his beer on the ledge.

"You alone, boy?" the Leatherman asked.

"Yes, Sir. I'm here alone."

"You aren't now." With that, the Leatherman firmly gripped the boy's right shoulder and pushed him down to his knees.

"Show respect to your Sir, boy."

The boy bent over and kissed the toe of the Leatherman's left boot.

"Lick it, boy."

The boy tentatively licked the toe of the left boot and proceeded to lick the shaft of the boot.

"You call that worship, boy?" as the Leatherman reared his left boot upward into the boy's face.

The Leatherman repositioned the boy flat against the wall, still in a kneeling position, and heaved his boot into the face of the boy. The boy had no choice but to tongue the sole and toe of the boot.

"That's better, boy. Come with me, boy," the Leatherman ordered. As if led on an invisible leash, the Leatherman led the way through the bar to a back room. He sat down in the single chair and motioned for the boy down on the floor.

The boy began a more complete tonguing of the boot. After the Leatherman was satisfied, he lifted the right boot into the boy's face and the process began all over again.

As the boy licked the right boot, he felt the sting of the Leatherman's flogger against his back. The floggings increased in intensity.

Once he finished, the Leatherman leaned down into the boy's face and pronounced, "You're coming with me. I need a fuck boy for the night."

The man pulled a length of black bondage rope off of the same D ring and quickly tied the boy's hands behind him.

He led the boy out of the bar and into his car.

The ride was silent, punctuated only by the Leatherman's lighting of a big, thick cigar and his exhaling of the cigar's smoke.

The car drove through a tangle of streets until they arrived at a townhouse. The Leatherman unlocked the door and pushed the boy inside.

He led the boy downstairs to his extensive dungeon set-up.

"Shuck your clothes and then stand against the St. Andrew's cross, boy." The boy complied and was quickly restrained tightly into place.

The Leatherman removed his Muir cap and put on an executioner's hood. He hooded the boy too.

Without warning, the straps of the flogger hit the naked flesh of the boy's back, shoulders and ass.

The Leatherman was relentless in his flogging. Never stopping, increasing in intensity as each flogging crisscrossed the flogged areas.

The boy was feeling the pain and began moaning.

"Shut the fuck up!" the Leatherman ordered as he increased the floggings. It was as if he had four hands, the floggings were coming with increased brutality.

The boy's back was soon bloody and raw. The Leatherman repositioned the boy so that his chest was now the recipient of the lashings.

The Leatherman attached a pair of murderous alligator clamps to the boy's nips, weighted with extra weights.

He added a parachute with weights to the boy's cock and balls. The floggings continued until the boy's chest was covered with bloody marks.

The Leatherman twisted and pulled on the boy's tits and his cock and balls.

The boy was in agony, thinking, "Please stop, Sir."

"You had enough, boy?" the Leatherman asked.

"Yes, Sir. Thank you, Sir."

"I have just begun, boy." the Leatherman responded as he laughed sadistically.

He proceeded with more of the same. The session continued long into the night until the boy's head lolled to one side. He was left in this tortured condition for the rest of the night as the Leatherman retired upstairs.

The boy finally fell asleep in that position, his body aching and throbbing from the abuse.

The Leathermaster returned the following morning. The boy was sagging in his restraints but would soon be woken by the additional lashings the Leathermaster was about to administer. The boy's chest was crisscrossed with dried blood and the lashing marks. The Leatherman traced his gloved hand over some of the longest lashmarks. He nodded his head in approval at the work he had accomplished. He was a true sadist.

He took some pictures of his own work for his photo album. He would later number them as "Anonymous Boy #47".

He started the flogging slowly, to awaken the boy. The boy's head snapped upward as the first hard lashes hit his aching chest. The lashes hit his shoulders, his tits which were numb from the alligators which had remained in place all night. Particularly painful were the lashes he received to his stretched balls and cock, still weighted with the parachute. He attempted to scream but the Leathermaster had placed a ballgag in his mouth.

The abuse continued for several hours, the hooded Leatherman getting rock hard from watching the boy in pain.

The boy's lashmarks had crusted over during the night but had reopened with the fresh lashings.

The Leathermaster repositioned the boy and continued the abuse on the boy's aching back and ass.

The Leathermaster rubbed his own cock through the Leather pouch in which it was residing. It didn't remain there long before the Leathermaster pulled it out and massaged it. Pre-cum appeared in the piss slit as he thrust it up the boy's hole. His cock was aroused, exploring new territory. His cock quickly came, shooting a load of jism up the boy's aching ass.

Repositioning his cock in the Leather cod, the Leatherman whispered into the boy's ear, "Maybe next time when your Sir gives you freedom, you won't be so eager to explore."

The Leathermaster took the boy down from the St. Andrew's Cross and threw the boy's clothes toward him. He escorted the boy to the foyer and told him to find his own way home. The inner door slammed before the boy had a chance to respond. The boy redressed slowly and painfully, his tortured body sensitive to the clothes he was putting on in the hallway of the townhouse. He stumbled out into the cold morning air. He walked several blocks before hailing a taxi. The boy retrieved his car and drove home. He pulled the tee shirt off his bloodied body. He cleaned the bloody marks and fell into bed, where he slept for the next twelve hours. He was due to arrive at his Sir's house by 9:00 am the following morning.

It was only now that the boy pondered the comment made by the LeatherMaster as the session ended. As he continued to wait for his Sir's return, he questioned silently, "Did they know one another?" "Was I set up?"

The lashmarks had disappeared on his chest, for the most part, but he hadn't bothered to look on his back and ass where the floggings were more intense. "Does my Sir know? Oh, shit, he must know." He twisted his head left and right, but could not see his back or ass.

The boy became more panicked, contemplating his Sir's reaction.

The boy began sweating, twisting and turning. He anticipated that his Daddy had already seen the healing lashmarks and knew the truth. "Why didn't I say something as soon as I arrived, before he had me take off my clothes? Before he strapped me to the wall? I really fucked up. What if he releases me? He surely knows I serve and worship him as my LeatherMaster. My only LeatherMaster..." The boy was practically in hysterics as he heard the cranking of the Leatherman's motorcycle pulling into the driveway.

He trembled. Tears welled up in his eyes as he heard the garage door open. Heavy boots marched into the garage and the door closed.

He attempted to speak but the ballgag in his mouth reduced it to a mumble. His LeatherMaster did not reply. He was soon aware of the LeatherMaster's cigar, filling the garage with its aromatic smell.

The boots shuffled across the floor until the boy sensed his LeatherMaster was standing in back of him. He attempted to turn his head, but his head was jerked forward and forced to lean against the wall.

The flogging began without warning. It was as if his LeatherMaster had a flogger in each hand, assaulting his back and ass in alternate strokes. Harder and harder. Until his head arched backward from the pain. It seemed to hit every healing mark. He could feel the flesh being reopened. Sweat, or blood, was trickling down his back.

The boy endured it. He knew he deserved it. He squeezed his eyes shut as tears streamed down his cheeks inside the hood.

"I deserve this. I deserve this," he silently thought.

Finally, the floggings stopped as the boy slumped forward. His arms and legs were being unmanacled. He was spun around and leaned against the garage wall. The ballgag was removed. The hood was slowly unlaced.

As his eyes adjusted to the brightness of the garage lighting, the boy saw two Leathermen standing before him.

His LeatherMaster stood to the right. He wore an executioner's hood. As if having double vision, a Leatherman in an executioner's hood stood beside his Sir. It was the same man who had flogged him over the weekend.

"So, boy, I've been told of your weekend. That amounts to a confession."

"Yes, Sir, I meant…" the boy began but he was too tongue-tied to say any more.

The boy was remanacled to the garage wall and was worked over by the two Leathermen for several hours. His body ached from the abuse.

His back and ass were bloodied by the end of the session.

As punishment, the boy now reports to two LeatherMasters for intense floggings. Yes, indeed, confession might have been good for the soul, but furthermore, might have spared a Leatherboy's ass and back.

COPFUCK

The Leatherman had arrived early, as was his usual practice. He had stowed his bondage rope, floggers and paddles near the tree where he intended to tie the submissive and work him over.

They had agreed to meet at 1:00 AM near the fountain in the secluded park. He ignored the signs which said the park closed at dusk as well as the sign which prohibited tobacco products in the park. A large Churchill clenched in his mouth attested to that. The Leatherman was in full Leather – cycle jacket, Muir cap, studded cod on his pants, Dehner boots, and his tight Damascus gloves. He leaned against a tree, his right foot propped up against the trunk. He rotated his cigar with his left hand and massaged his cod with the right hand.

He watched the lights on the expressway as they blurred past and the lights of the high rise as lights dimmed and people retired for the evening. His night was just beginning.

Patience was not one of his virtues (not that he was that virtuous to begin with).He had not worn a watch, instead choosing his studded wristbands. When he put them on, he rationalized, "They support my wrists when I'm flogging a boy's ass." He instinctively knew that the boy would be late so he brought a supply of cigars. Despite repeated warnings and floggings, this boy was always late.

The Leatherman continued to smoke and stroke.

He was becoming more irritated with the boy for keeping this Leatherman waiting. More lights continued to dim in the high rise.

Finally, he heard footsteps approaching.

"It's about time, boy…"

"What?…Who's there?" and with that a spotlight from a flashlight pierced my eyes.

As my eyes adjusted to the light, my brain rationalized that it was a cop. And it was.

"The park is closed after dusk. Hands where I can see them… What's your name?"

I complied with the two requests. As I handed him my driver's license, I could see that he was young and handsome.

As he continued to question me, I viewed a trim body fitting snuggly inside a blue uniform. His visored hat low on his forehead, but it couldn't hide the features of a nice-looking man. Tight Damascus gloves in place. Then, I looked down and saw the knee-high Dehners.

"Are you mounted patrol?"

"Normally," he answered, "I'm doing double duty tonight. Just answer my questions."

I complied.

"You know you're not supposed to be in the park and the park prohibits the use of tobacco products."

"I know, Officer, I just couldn't resist... a beautiful night like this and it's a brand of cigar I've never tried before. I'll just bet you are a cigar smoker."

"My old lady won't let me smoke in the house," he replied.

"Well, here's your chance...out under the stars. Who am I going to report you to, the cops?"

He chuckled momentarily. I reached for my cigar case and offered him a smoke, my clip, and a light.

"Thanks," as he took a long drag on it, "Damn, that's a good taste."

Just then my cellphone rang. It was my boy – reporting an accident on the freeway. He was at least forty minutes away. "All right, catch you another time."

The cop grinned, with a knowing look on his face. "Did you get stood up?"

"Looks like it."

"Now what are you gonna do?"

"Guess I'll go home unless you're going to arrest me."

"Maybe you'd like to arrest me, Sir."

I was startled. "Come again," I said.

"Ever since I joined mounted patrol, I get a hard-on when I put on these boots. Seeing you in full Leather, makes my cock salute."

I reached down and it was true – a hard cock pressed against the fabric of the police-issued trousers.

I unzipped his pants slowly and extracted a throbbing cock. He moaned as I massaged it with my gloved hands.

"That's some nightstick you've got, Officer."

I outlined the plan that I had devised for my boy and me.

"Yes, Sir, I'd like to be that boy."

"Aren't you still on duty?"

He checked the lighted dial of his watch and replied "Off duty ten minutes ago."

We walked to his patrol car and he radioed in. He explained as we walked to the patrol car that a number of the officers from the precinct were attending a funeral the next morning in New York State for a fallen officer. He was filling in. As we reached the patrol car, I realized that this could be entrapment, but I just felt that he was above board. As he talked to headquarters, I viewed a man with dark features, black short-cropped hair, a heavy five o'clock shadow, and the damned sexiest blue eyes. Muscular arms and a cute ass. He pulled his car to an unobtrusive area and he said, "I'm your boy."

We walked to my chosen tree. "You have the key to your handcuffs, son."

"Yes, Sir," he replied.

Handing me the handcuffs and the key, I secured his hands in back of the tree.

I slowly untied his tie and unbuttoned his shirt. His chest was covered in black fur, two pink nips hiding among all the black fur. I slowly massaged his pecs as I thought, "Wish I'd brought a razor. But a shaving scene can be a future activity."

"Oh, Sir, that feels so good."

I pinched his nipples with my gloved hands. He shuddered.

I increased the pressure on his nips. He moaned and twisted. I spread his shirt open, pulling it out of the trousers.

I pulled it off his shoulders and massaged them, with my gloved hands.

My studded cod pressed into his crotch area.

I leaned his head back against the trunk of the tree and thrust my tongue in his mouth. He responded – he was a damned good kisser.

His hands strained against the handcuffs – I know he wanted to caress my jaw to reciprocate my action.

With our tongues exploring one another's mouths, I reached down and unbuckled his trousers. They fell around his knees. I had already discovered that he was wearing no underwear. It made it far easier for me to grab his cock and balls and squeeze.

He moaned even more loudly.

I pressed my excited manmound into his and reached around, grabbing his asscheeks.

We continued kissing for some time, me alternately playing with nips, cock, balls and asscheeks.

I don't usually suck a boy's cock, but I knew I wanted to taste this one. I knelt down and took his throbbing rod in my mouth.

"Oh, Sir… Oh, Sir," he moaned. Within minutes, he shot a cumload down my throat and it tasted fucking great.

"Now, son, it's time to pay for Daddy's services."

I repositioned him so that he was now facing the tree, handcuffed.

I started slowly with my mild flogger. He apparently had never been flogged before, but I could tell that he was enjoying it. Arching his back and his ass to receive the series of floggings.

"Oh, Sir, thank you, Sir."

My floggings intensified. I switched to a heavy flogger and he responded well. He was enjoying it – I could tell from the soft moanings and expletives he occasionally omitted. In between floggings, I rubbed his back and ass with my gloved hands and massaged my own overly-excited cock.

As I massaged his ass, I explored his hole with my gloved hands. He moaned softly. I maneuvered his handcuffed hands closer to the base of the tree and spread his legs. My cock had hardened considerably in its pouch and I knew that it was time for it to enjoy some fresh territory. I unsnapped the cod and eased it up the boy's hole. His asscheeks tightened.

I slapped them, telling him to 'Relax'.

My cock thrust into his boyhole and I began pumping. My balls were slapping against his asscheeks. I reached around and pulled on his nips. Squeezing and pinching. Pumping.

As I achieved a frenzied pumping, the boy let out a healthy scream which I quickly stifled with a gloved hand over his mouth.

It wasn't long before I shot a healthy load of cum.

For what I assume was a first-time novice, he did really well. I told him so.

"Thank you, Sir," he replied.

I took the handcuffs off his right wrist and ordered him to kneel. I then handcuffed his hands behind his back.

With his face pressed in my crotch, I left nothing to his imagination as to what I wanted him to do. He did it expertly. My dick received a delicious tonguing. He kept eating more and more of it. Don't know how he did it, but he also took my balls in one mouthful.

I soon jacked off for a second time, this time in his handsome mouth, and he continued to lick my cock until it was clean.

"Sir, I better get going... my old lady will worry." I released the handcuffs from his left wrist, but quickly positioned his hands around the tree once again and secured the handcuffs.

"You'll go when I say you go, boy. Your Daddy isn't through with you."

A healthy scream was pre-empted by my gloved hand over his mouth. He struggled but I pressed my body against his. His protests soon turned to passionate and frenzied man-to-man action. Our cocks felt the heat of one another's cock, both quickly responding.

My black Leather skins ground into his copflesh. I replaced my gloved hand with my mouth and we kissed, my hands now firmly clamped on either side of his jaw. Our cocks were throbbing next to each other's, both hard and ready to pump. And we did, cop juice and Leatherman's juice intermingled. We were both sweating from the exertion as we finally separated.

Releasing him, I handed him his regulation handcuffs with the key. He fell to his knees and thanked me for the evening.

It was the first of many sessions. But we have subsequently met at the bondage tree instead of the fountain for nights of homomasculine pleasure.

In those subsequent sessions, however, I have always worn my cop's uniform. Tan Leather with a California Highway Patrol patch on each shoulder. Sam Browne belt. Spitshined Dehners. He always wears his mounted patrol uniform, even though he knows he is the one to be mounted, flogged, and tortured.

There is a thin line between real life and fantasy, especially in the brotherhood of cops. And, incidentally, I also wear a cop's uniform during the day. I'm a New Jersey cop, off duty the night he and I first met. Guess I should tell him that at some point.

FUCK THE TRUCKER

Tony was on one of his usual truck runs, a three-day stint from New York to Florida. It was the busiest season, right before Christmas. Tony was a slender young man of twenty-four. He had started working for his old man when he turned sixteen and had worked his way up to the vice president of the company. And, even though he was the vice president, he often had to fill in on runs when he did not have enough drivers. He didn't mind, he enjoyed being on the open road. It led to a lot of masculine, sexual adventures.

His old man was a biker and Tony had grown up around well-muscled truckers who enjoyed riding their cycles in their spare time. His old man was tough, no doubt about it. He had raised Tony to fend for himself, teaching Tony boxing techniques, for instance. Tony usually landed on his ass with one swat from the old man, but Tony had learned to get right back up and punch his dad. His dad probably let him take the punch. Tony had never seen his dad in anything but his cycle Leathers and Tony had grown up with a lot of fantasies about Leathermen.

When Tony had turned twenty-one, his old man had proved to be a generous father by giving Tony a cycle. Since that time, Tony rode with his dad's biker buddies, who usually rode with a Leather-clad woman on the back. "What I really want is a stud in tight pants, with his cock pressing against my butt," Tony thought, but he never expressed it to his super macho dad.

Tony was stopped at a stoplight and he viewed his surroundings. It was well after midnight and he had to drive at least three more hours before finishing his day, to stay on schedule. His old man was strict about schedules.

He looked over to the adjoining property and viewed a man standing on the steps of a small outbuilding. A streetlight highlighted the man who stood on the steps. Tony's eyes practically popped out of his head when he viewed a muscular man in a black Leather harness, black chaps and a beautiful cock hanging down between his legs. The man was whipping his cock and balls with a Leather whip and pulling on his nipples with the other Leather gloved hand.

"Jesus," Tony moaned as a horn blasted, bringing him back to reality. He quickly accelerated, but he watched the Leatherman until completely out of view. He made a mental note of the location and promised himself to investigate the next time he was through this route. Fortunately for him, he was through this area frequently. For the rest of the drive, he fantasized about the man as he quickly memorized every creamy detail.

As it turned out, Bob called in a week later with an injury and could not do his run. Tony had to fill in. It was the eve of his twenty-fifth birthday. He would spend his birthday on the road. "No big deal," he thought as he dragged on a cigarette.

As he once again approached the area, he mentally calculated the exact location.

"Here," he thought, "No, that's not right…"

"Shit," he muttered as he sailed past what he thought was the intersection.

"No, wait, it's still up ahead."

He pulled off to the side of the highway to get his bearings. "No, it's still ahead…I think," as he cursed himself for not writing more details down. After all, he traveled thousands of miles in a year. "No, I think this is it right ahead." He once again pulled to the side of the road.

"Thank you, Trucker God" because there to the right was the outbuilding and "Thank you, again!" as he viewed the Leatherman standing on the steps. The man was once again in his black Leather harness, chaps, and black Leather gloves. The man was watching Tony and he briefly waved his whip in the air before returning to his personal flogging.

Tony dismounted his truck's cab and pretended to check a tire. He glanced up and the man had returned to whipping his cock. The Leatherman knew that he had hooked the young boy and soon, the boy would find some excuse for approaching him. The boy lit a cigarette and looked around before marching across the strip of land which separated him from the handsome specimen of Leatherhood.

"Excuse me, Sir…"

The Leatherman ignored the boy and continued his whipping.

"Aaah, excuse me, Sir… I wonder if you could…"

"Shut up, boy," the Leatherman growled, "Get down onto your knees and worship my cock…"

Tony needed no further invitation as he fell to his knees and took the man's throbbing manrod in his mouth. The man began whipping the boy's flannel shirted back. The sensation was incredible and something he had never experienced until now.

"Get down on that dick, boy."

Tony swallowed the man's cock, inch by inch until he had the whole manrod in his willing mouth and throat.

The Leatherman pulled the boy's head closer to his crotch and the boy experienced the powerful aroma of a real Leatherman's body. The man's chaps fit tightly around each muscular calf and thigh. His harness fit tightly over his beautiful, sexy chest.

Tony kept sucking until the man's body began pounding the cock further into his mouth and soon, the man shot a load down the willing boy's throat.

After the man had creamed and sighed a deep sigh, he pulled the boy roughly up by his flannel shirt.

"In, boy" and the man dragged the boy inside his tool shed.

The tool shed was not outfitted with the usual assortment of saws and drills. A large table with black Leather padding and straps on each side of the table greeted his eyes.

Tony's cock was hard at the thought of being strapped down to the table and he was soon in that position.

The Leatherman pulled a black Leather hood off a nearby table and soon all Tony could see were a pair of piercing blue eyes and the Leatherman's mouth. The man lighted a long, black cigar and began slapping the boy with his gloved black hands. At first, it was pleasant, but as he continued slapping the boy's tender flesh, the boy began to resist the Master's slapping. The Leatherman tightened the straps, making the boy immobile. He also added a Leather blindfold to cover the boy's eyes.

The slapping continued until the boy's body was tenderized, red all over. At times, it felt like there were two pairs of hands slapping his ass.

The man stood at the end of the table, removing his glove. He produced a container of lube and greased up his right hand.

Before the boy could protest, a fist was inserted up his virgin ass. The sensation hurt, of course, but the boy's fantasies were coming true and he quickly shifted into enjoying this man's pleasures.

The man's fist continued to explore the boy's hole, but it was abruptly withdrawn. What seemed like an even bigger fist was inserted and soon was exploring the very edges of the boy's hole.

The boy was not quite aware that the man had placed heavy Leather shackling cuffs on his wrists and was hoisting the boy until he was kneeling on the black Leather table. The boy's hands were suspended above his head. The Leatherman pulled a heavy black wooden paddle off the wall and pretty soon the "WHACK!" of the paddle of the tender young ass was heard. The boy flinched at each paddling. The paddling was coming from two different directions and it was apparent that someone had joined the Leatherman in the boy beating. The paddling continued until the boy passed out.

When the boy awoke, sunshine streamed in through the toolshed's window. The blindfold had been removed. The boy attempted to move, but he was heavily shackled to the table. His body ached from the abuse he had received. "Shit," he thought, "I gotta get on the road... my old man will kill me, if I'm not on schedule." His futile attempts to escape were useless.

Just then, the door swung open and a handsome Leatherman strutted in. He was dressed in the usual attire. His black Leather had been freshly oiled as had the man's chest. The man's head was covered in a black Leather hood.

Despite his sore body, the boy got an immediate hard on.

"Had a good night, did you son?"

"Whaaatt? What did you say?"

The Leatherman repeated his question, but the voice was different. The boy was still groggy from the rough night, but there was something familiar in the voice.

"I was wondering how long it would take you to find Jim's rest stop. He and I have been fuckbuddies for years. Why do you think I always came back with a smile on my face."

With that, the Leatherman removed his hood. It was Tony's father. His fuckbuddy Jim walked in and the two proceeded to work their willing boy over for most of the day. The hell with the schedule. After all, it was the boy's birthday.

This story originally appeared in
The Flagship, Summer 2005 (Issue #67)

THE ANSWER

The Leatherman met the submissive over the internet and a session had been scheduled for the weekend which was now at hand. The submissive was ordered to appear at 3 PM on Saturday, and for once, the boy had not backed out. Or at least, he hadn't given his new-found Master an excuse for not coming. The workover room was in readiness for an intense S&M session of flogging and bondage.

The Leathermaster sat in full Leather on his back porch after a morning of weeding the seeming jungle that had arisen on his extensive property. As he waited for the submissive to appear, the Leatherman viewed the lawn which was in need of trimming and the weeds which were still in need of pulling amidst the extensive plantings on his property. Maybe he should make the sub do some yard work. After all, his ad for a gardener had produced no results in the three weeks it had appeared in the paper. The Leatherman had better luck with his appeal on the internet for sexslaves. He had enjoyed good success with finding submissive boys to service his mancock.

The submissive was older than most of the boys that the Daddy routinely worked over, however, he had begged and pleaded with the Leathermaster until the man had finally granted the boy a session.

"Better not fuck up, boy," the Leathermaster had sternly warned the submissive.

A truck pulled into the yard of the Daddy's private property and the submissive exited the cab.

He was even older than his photos indicated. In fact, the photos looked nothing like the boy who now presented himself for sex. "Hell, they seldom do," the Leatherman mused. However, the boy was in boots, blue jeans and a white tee shirt as ordered. The boy lowered his eyes as he approached the backporch.

"Sir, I am here…"

"Shut up and get down on your knees…"

The boy looked uncertain, however, dropped to his knees when the Leatherdaddy yelled, "NOW!"

The man motioned for the boy to crawl up the steps. The boy lay at the man's booted feet.

The Leatherman rested his feet on the boy's back.

The boy said nothing as the man continued to stoke his cigar and roughly pushed the boy's body 180 degrees until the boy's willing ass was pointed toward the man. The Leatherman pulled the boy's jeans down around his thighs and rested a booted foot on each asscheek. He spread the asscheeks further apart and pulled a dildo off a nearby table. He quickly greased it up with lube and shoved it up the boy's ass. The boy began to protest, but took the dildo without comment as the man's booted foot pushed it further up the boy's willing hole.

"You keep that in place, boy."

"Yes, Sir."

Just to make sure the boy complied, the man rested his right booted foot on the dildo's base.

The Leathermaster pulled a large flogger off the table and began flogging the boy's back. The floggings increased in intensity and as the boy momentarily flinched from each lash, the man pushed the dildo in further and further into the boy's hole.

He continued to lash the boy until the boy's back was obscured by the fresh markings.

The Daddy pulled his feet away and grabbed the boy under the armpits. He positioned the boy so that he was leaning over the porch railing.

"Sir, you don't understand..." The Leatherman roughly shoved a dildo plug in his boy's mouth.

The boy remained in position as the Leathermaster removed the dildo from the boy's ass, pulled out his own mancock and replaced the dildo with his manrod in the boy's hole. The boy groaned, but made no further comment.

The Daddy pounded his cock into the boy's hole. His balls were encased in a bull ball bag and that slapped against the boy's flesh as the cock explored the willing hole.

"Please, Sir..." the boy mumbled with the plug in his mouth, but the man ignored the pleading as he became more excited and his hardened cock hardened even more.

While he continued to pound his manflesh into the submissive's ass, the Leathermaster reached over and pulled the boy's hands behind his back. Heavy Leather wrist restraints were buckled and then locked into place.

"But, Sir, I was just..." were the boy's words as he struggled to talk with the plug in his mouth.

The bull bag swung back and forth, slapping the boy's asscheeks and the man's thighs. It was a delicious feeling and despite the man's resolve not to shoot, just to reach near climax and then withdraw, his cock had a mind of its own and soon pumped a load of jism up his fuckslave's ass.

He withdrew his cock, dripping with cum and repositioned the boy on his knees. The boy's head was pushed down in order that he could clean off his man's tool. The Leatherman removed the plug.

"Sir," the boy trembled, but continued, "I don't want the job."

The man laughed, "Can't handle it, huh, boy?"

"Sir, I was just responding to the ad for a gardener. I really need a job, but if this is the way you treat your gardener... I don't think I'm interested!"

HAMMOCKS ARE FOR A MAN AND HIS BOY

All was in readiness in the playroom, as the Leatherman sat down on his back porch to await the arrival of a boy. The Leatherman was in his codpieced pants and his Wesco crotch-high boots. Encased in his black Leather Damascus gloves, his left hand struck a match to the end of a freshly-clipped cigar while his right hand rotated the cigar for an even lighting. The boy arrived two minutes early for his appointment. The boy emerged from his Honda Civic in the prescribed outfit – a white tee shirt, blue jeans, and boots. The boy looked nervously in the direction of the Leatherman as he crossed the yard.

"Hi, Sir," he said, as he waved his hand and approached the porch. The boy was a recent addition to the Leather chat line and apparently did not have much experience in greeting a Leatherdaddy.

The man simply motioned to the floor between his Wesco boot-covered legs.

The boy did not immediately catch on to the hand signal as he stood in front of the man. The man tugged on the waistband of the boy's jeans, pulling the boy toward him. He then unceremoniously pushed the boy down to his knees. He repositioned the boy squarely between his two booted feet. The boy's head was yanked forward until the boy's mouth was touching the man's studded codpiece.

"Clean my codpiece, boy," the Leatherdaddy commanded.

The boy began licking the codpiece, tonguing the metal studs and the Leather on which they were positioned. The Daddy held the boy's head firmly in place until the boy had licked and sucked the entire surface of the cod. The Daddy then manipulated the boy's mouth to the left corner snap of the cod. The boy needed little instruction for the unsnapping of the man's codpiece.

"Suck, boy."

The boy needed even less instruction on the sucking of a man's cock and soon was happily slurping the man's shaft and low hanging balls.

The man's cock hardened quickly. Within about twenty minutes, the man's cock released a healthy load of cum down the boy's throat.

"Good, boy. You've done well for the first time and deserve a bit of relaxation for your efforts." The Daddy drew the boy toward him and jammed his tongue down the boy's throat. They engaged in a long tonguing, the Daddy roughly pulling the boy's head toward him with his gloved hand.

Eventually the Daddy pushed the boy away and ordered him to follow the Leatherman. The boy followed willingly. The Daddy's hammock was set up in the back yard.

The Daddy climbed in and positioned his legs spread eagle. His Wescos looked handsome, stretched out to their full length. His cockbulge pointing toward the sky.

The boy started to crawl in, but the Daddy said, "Not so fast, son. Take off your clothes."

The boy pulled his tee shirt off, revealing a nice set of tits. He bent over to unlace his boots and the Leatherman slapped the boy's ass. "Hurry up, boy."

The boy quickly pulled off his boots, followed by his jeans. They were discarded in a pile on the lawn. His dick was nice and hard. The Daddy played with it for a few minutes with his vicelike hands, but released it so that the boy could snuggle into the hammock with his Daddy.

The boy lay his head on his Daddy's shoulder and the two fondled for quite a while. The sun, directly overhead, produced a healthy mansweat on both the man and his boy.

The boy settled in next to the Leatherman. The man caressed the boy's head and soon, the boy fell asleep.

The boy's right hand settled on the man's chest, massaging the man's nips absently while the boy slept. The Leatherman stuck one gloved finger at a time into the boy's mouth and the boy tongued each finger in turn while he continued to sleep.

The Daddy stoked his cigar and played absently with his cockmound.

He pulled open his codpiece and his cock pointed heavenward.

The Daddy removed the boy's hand from his chest and positioned it around the base of his own cock. The boy's hand massaged the cock while he continued to sleep. With the attention received, the man's healthy cock hardened, growing in girth and length.

The two remained in that position for some time, until the boy abruptly rolled over in his sleep.

He presented to the Daddy a very inviting ass, soft as a baby's bottom.

"This is too good an opportunity," the Daddy thought.

The Leatherman lubricated his mandick with a layer of sweat and spit, rolled over on his left hip, and inserted his cock between the boy's asscheeks.

Unfortunately, that action shifted the weight of the hammock. The boy rolled out of the hammock. The Daddy, with his cock in the boy's ass, tumbled out after him, landing the man squarely on top of his boy. The boy woke up with an "Ummpph" as the man landed on top of him. The man's cock was rammed further into the boy's hole.

The man began a frenzied pumping into the boy's hole. His sweaty body and the boy's sweat acted as a natural lubricant. The man began sliding up and down, up and down, along the boy's back. The boy's asscheeks widened as the fully awakened boy accepted the man's cock into his willing hole.

As his cock became more aroused, the man began a labored breathing as he pounded his manrod into the boy's fuckhole.

Sweat was dripping off his forehead onto the boy's back.

He reached underneath the boy and twisted the boy's nips.

The frenzied pumping continued.

Gliding back and back against the small of the boy's back, their sweats intermingling, the Daddy was beginning to moan with pleasure. His dick was gathering cum from every corner of his masculine body for a massive release.

The man arched his body and spreadeagled his legs. He grabbed the boy's hands and extended them fully, interlocking his gloved fingers with that of the boy's. He lay squarely on top of the boy. The boy was moaning with pleasure, his own hardened cock buried beneath him in the grass. The boy arched his ass upwards, allowing the man's Leathercock to maneuver in the boyhole more deeply.

Both man and boy were sweating profusely.

The man began gasping as he reached closer and closer to climax. The boy was moaning. The man's body was tenderizing the boy's entire body with its power and strength.

The man knew he could hold his cockload no longer. He accelerated the ramming of the cock and with a mighty shouted "FUCK!!!" he shot an immense load of cum up the boy's hole.

He collapsed on top of the boy whose ass continued to expand and contract, expand and contract, squeezing the juice out of his man's cock.

As soon as he recovered, the man rolled the boy over and began tonguing the boy's mouth. The boy's cock was throbbing. The Daddy's cum-soaked dick lay right beside the boy's cock. Within minutes, the boy's cock shot, spreading even more jism on the two bodies. The man and boy continued to fuck and suck for some time before retiring to the toolshed for Session Two.

The hammock remained overturned until the next day when the Leatherman brought another boy to the hammock for the same activity.

"What a great Labor Day this has been…" the Leatherman thought, as he lighted a fresh cigar and thrust his cock into the willing boy's hole.

FLOGGING BY CANDLELIGHT

The boy was in full black Leather and lying face up, as ordered. His gloved hands and booted feet were tied to each of the corners of the four-postered bed. The boy wore a black Leather hood over his head – the eyes covered with a blindfold. The mouth was gagged with a snap-on gag. The boy was comfortably situated, however, with a Leather pillow under his head. He awaited the Leatherman with patience. The Leatherman had a meeting to attend, but would return shortly for a satisfying session.

The boy's hearing was muted by the hood, but after a period, he heard the Leatherman enter the room. The man bent down and rubbed the boy's head. He slapped the boy softly on the cheek and whispered something indiscernible. The boy's ears strained, but nothing could be heard for several more minutes. The Leatherman was changing out of his white collar shit suit and tie, discarded on a nearby chair. He selected his heaviest Leather pants with a spiked cod. He pulled on his spit-shined Dehners and pulled on his tight Damascus gloves. To complete the uniform, a Muir cap was pulled down to his forehead.

The man stood looking at the handsome youth for a long second. The boy's body was slender, but a nice set of pecs and a decent bulge in the pants was evident. It would be even more evident within a few short seconds as the man crawled onto the bed and covered the boy's body with his own. He began a stimulating massage of the boy's arms, reaching down to circle the boy's nipples through the Leather shirt with his gloved hands. He repeated this until the boy was responding with a slight sigh from his plugged mouth. The Leatherman's cod, in its extended pouch, lay parallel to the boy's hardening cock.

He rubbed the boy's cheeks and patted the top of the boy's head. The boy could feel the sweet caresses of his Master through the Leather hood. The Master continued to rub the boy's arm and chest, reaching down occasionally to playfully tug at the boy's codpiece. The boy's cock hardened at the touch of his Leatherman's gloved hands. The boy could feel his Leatherman's cock harden within the Leather codpiece his Daddy wore. The boy began to think of servicing the cock, his tongue licking up and down the shaft and swallowing the head of the cock. He began moaning with the thought of this pleasure. He knew he had to be patient, a load of cum down his throat would be his reward for his patience.

"Sir," he thought, "you are the best Daddy in the world…"

The Leatherman continued to massage his boy's body with his – the feel of Leather against Leather was so fucking erotic and he wanted to prolong it as long as he could.

He reached down and unsnapped the boy's shirt one snap at a time. His gloved hands reached in and squeezed each nipple with a gloved hand. The boy had very sensitive tits and he flinched as his Daddy squeezed. The Leatherman rubbed the boy's chest with his gloved hands. The Leatherman reached up, raising the boy's head and unsnapped the gag. He inserted his tongue into the boy's willing mouth and they kissed for a long time as the Leatherman continued to rub his Leathered body against the boy's.

"What do you want, boy?" the Leatherman asked.

"To please you, Sir. In any way I can."

"Good answer, boy," as the Leatherman continued to caress his boy.

He slowly unzipped the boy's pants and worked them down around the boy's knees.

The Leatherman reached under the boy's left leg and began squeezing the boy's asscheek. He rubbed the 'dividing line' between the cheeks and then massaged the other. The Daddy reached over to the bedside table and retrieved a Leather dildo, extremely flexible after many uses.

He lubricated it with his own spit and spreading the boy's asscheeks, jammed it up the boy's rectum. The boy moaned, twisted, and turned as the dildo made its way up his hole. The man held his knee against the base of the dildo so that the boy's ass could not reject it. The man leaned over and grabbed the boy's dick and balls in his Leathered hand. He squeezed them hard, separating the ball sac with his thumb and positioning the four remaining fingers on the shaft of the cock. The Daddy's hand was like a vice and the boy's cock hardened until it was pulsing in the man's iron grip.

The Leatherman reached over with his other hand and pinched the boy's nipple. The boy flinched as the power of the vice-like grip translated into pain. The man increased the intensity with his left hand on the boy's right nipple, his right hand on the boy's cock and balls, and the knee holding the dildo in place.

After working the nipple for a few minutes, he transferred his attentions to the other nip.

The boy was enjoying the session and his whole body was feeling relaxed and aroused.

The Daddy had other plans for the scene to change, however.

He stepped away from the bed momentarily and selected a Leather paddle.

Without warning, he lifted the boy's ass and struck it repeatedly with great intensity. The boy flinched as the first whack of the paddle hit his ass. He continued flinching, attempting to pull his body away from the paddlings.

"LIE STILL, BOY," the Leatherman commanded. The authoritative voice came through the Leather hood loud and clear.

It was hard for the boy to obey as the Leather paddle assaulted his ass.

The Daddy continued, rubbing his swollen cockhead which had appeared above the cod. He was a true sadomasochist and enjoyed inflicting pain on his subject. He knew that this boy could take it. With each session he had enjoyed with this boy, he had increased the levels of pain.

He next pulled his heavy flogger off the D ring of his tight Leather pants.

He removed the wrist and ankle restraints off the right side of the boy's body and rolled his boy on his side. The Leatherman proceeded to flog the boy's back until crisscrossed red marks appeared on his sub's back.

The sub was breathing heavily, his body tightening with each additional flogging.

Conversely, the Leatherman was feeling extremely relaxed, taking out his day's aggression on the boy's hide.

The flogger continued its assault on the boy as the man reached with his left and grabbed the boy's cock and balls in a vicelike grip. The dick had shrunk, but as the Daddy's gloved hands pulled on the boy's privates, they swelled to a reasonable size.

The floggings stopped as the Daddy placed an English cock harness around each nut and the base of the boy's cock. The Daddy pinched the loose skin of each segment of the ballsac and the cock. It hurt like hell and the boy screamed.

Daddy's right gloved hand reached up and pinched the boy's nostrils and covered the boy's mouth with the palm of his hand.

The boy lost consciousness.

As the Leatherman carried the boy downstairs, slung lightly over his broad shoulder, he formed a mental list of all the boys he had taken into the basement. He had only been in this house about six years and it had taken him some time to set up his dungeon. And he had a number of repeat boys who had serviced his cock with respect and submissiveness. This boy was number 20? 21?

The boy woke sometime later to find himself spread-eagle on a Leather-covered table in the dungeon. He was naked. Legs and wrists tightly strapped into place. The plug was back in the boy's mouth. The boy's body was tingling and as his senses returned his whole body felt different. Raising his head as best he could, he squinted through the eyeholes of the hood. The Leatherman held a lighted candle over the boy's torso.

"You awake, boy?"

The boy could only nod "Yes". His torso was being covered in the drippings of hot wax. With every sweep of the Leather gloved hand, the boy's dick was being assaulted by a single drop of wax. It stung momentarily, but at the same time was oddly stimulating. The boy's cock arched upward as if a moth to the flame.

"GOOD BOY," the Leatherman commented as he left another trail of hot wax up the boy's torso and around the nipples.

As the boy continued to process information, it was apparent that the Leatherman had shaved the boy's torso and pubic area for the receipt of the hot wax.

The Leatherman continued the process. He stopped momentarily to extract a cigar from his cigar case, clip it, light it with the burning candle, and draw on the cigar heavily. He was now so relaxed that he wanted the session to continue indefinitely. He continued to leave a trail of wax up and down the boy's torso, always administering one drop on the boy's hardened cock.

The Leatherman continued for some time. He pulled out a fresh razor and shaved off the hair around the boy's tender nipples. After doing so, he began a concentrated effort of encircling the nips with a ring of hotwax. Occasionally, a drop of wax would drip on the tip of the nipple, extracting a moan from the boy. Each time the boy moaned, a fresh dripping of wax would hit his cock. The Leatherman reached up and rubbed the boy's shoulders and then tweaked his nipples. The wax had formed a hardened casing, but the boy still felt the touch of his Master's gloved hands on the nips. The boy moaned with pleasure.

The wax assault continued until the boy's nips, line down to the navel, and his cock were encrusted in wax.

Releasing the restraints, the Leatherman ordered the boy on his knees.

He released his mancock from the cod and ordered the waxed boy to suck his Master's dick. He removed the mouth plug.

The boy willingly complied, he worshipped the man's cock.

The Leatherman pulled the boy's head closer to the base of his cock and thrust it repeatedly in and out of the receptive hole of the boy's hood.

The Leatherman's balls slapped against the boy's chin as he fucked the boy's mouth.

It wasn't long before he shot a load of thick, rich cum down the willing boy's throat.

The boy gratefully licked the cum from around his mouth.

"Thank you, Master."

"We're not through, boy."

With that, he escorted the boy to the St. Andrew's cross and bound his wrists and ankles to the cross.

He proceeded to do an intense flogging on the boy's naked back and ass. It was already marked with the Leatherman's earlier floggings.

The boy wrenched against his arm restraints as the floggings became more brutal in intensity.

This was one of the longest sessions the Leatherman and his boy had had. The wax was stiffening on the boy's torso and cock, hurting when he jerked from the floggings, but his nipples felt comfortable in their encasing of wax.

It was almost as if the Leatherman knew what the boy was thinking. Removing a pair of alligator clamps, he placed them on the nipples and pressed the boy's body against the wooden cross.

"AAAHHH," the boy screamed.

"Take it, boy," the Leatherman commanded.

He added the pressure of his own gloved hands on the nipple clamps and the boy screamed in pain.

"I said, take it, boy," the Leatherman snarled, as he angrily slapped the boy's right cheek.

The Leatherman once again pinched the clamps and pulled on the chain connecting the two clamps. The boy wrenched from side to side, increasing the pull of the clamps.

The Leatherman continued flogging the boy until the boy quieted down. With quiet resignation, he would have to accept his Master's pain as part of his initiation into the boyhood of Leather sadomasochism.

With this thought, the boy apparently received a boost of adrenaline and began to crave the next beating. The Master willingly complied, flogging the boy in a frenzied beating. Abruptly, they stopped.

The Leatherman's cock was once again hardened by the action. He lubed up his cock and without warning, shoved it up the boy's hole for a final assault. It was only a few minutes later that he pumped his jism into the boy's ass.

"Damn," the Leatherman thought, "that felt great. Hope the boy enjoyed it."

He released the boy from his restraints and the boy dropped gratefully to his knees. He licked his Master's cock until the residue was gone.

The Leatherman escorted the boy over to the workover table, but instead of ordering his boy to lie on it, began the process of cleaning the boy up. He swabbed the areas gently and removed the wax without inflicting any more pain.

"Thank you, Master. Sir, when can we do this session again?" the boy begged.

"My decision, boy," was the only response the Leatherman gave his boy as they headed upstairs.

A heavy, black flogger, not used for the above scene, began twitching. The Leatherman sent a telepathic message to the flogger, to be 'ready for action'. What the boy didn't suspect is that the Leatherman had determined that their next session should begin as soon as he manacled the boy to the bed once again.

BULL RING

"Sir, may I lick your boot, Sir?"

The message was one of my many messages on a Leather site that I viewed frequently. I noted that the submissive lived several states away. I responded with a polite thank you and a "Sure, son" and thought no more about it. Several days passed before I received the same message. Persistence pays off and so, by the fourth message bearing the same question, I took the boy's offer a little more seriously.

I looked at the boy's profile. I expected to see an average looking guy with some kinky tendencies. Instead, a handsome, muscular hunk was the writer of the message. Shaved head, big beefy arms, six-pack. His profile indicated that he was 100% passive.

My return response was friendlier, more enticing. Suggestive, alluring.

He began to message me daily, inquiring politely which boots I was wearing.

Wesco crotch-high. Military. Dehners. Cowboy boots. Whatever mood I was in.

The ones that seemed to illicit an immediate response were the Wesco crotch-highs, laced up to my studded cod with black boot laces. I wear them frequently. They feel so damned good. I often take walks in full Leather, through snow, mud, rain, slop. They get dirty and my Wescos were in need of servicing.

I finally instructed the boy, if he was serious, to visit for a particular weekend. He would be expected to service my boots, my cock, and the Leatherman associated with them.

He responded to the affirmative.

At the beginning of the week, I wrote, "Still coming, boy?" As the weekend approached, I kept waiting for him to respond.

Finally, Thursday afternoon his email came, "Sir, may I lick your boot, Sir?"

I gave him instructions on where, when, and what I expected.

"Sir, yes, Sir," was his response.

It was a mid-July weekend. Hot and humid. Saturday afternoon arrived and I was suited up. Full Leather. I relished the sweatiness of being in full Leather even on the hottest day of the year. Crotch-highs in place. Floggers on my D ring. Gloves. Muir cap.

Almost to the millisecond of his anticipated arrival, a car pulled into my driveway. I took a deep breath and stood at the top of the steps, spreading my legs with the toes of the boots pointing outward.

The candidate emerged from his car. Mirrored sunglasses. Shaved head. No facial hair. Shirtless. Big, rippling abs. Washboard stomach. Titrings. Leather armbands on his muscular arms. Narrow waist. Leather pants. Cowboy boots. And one detail that I had not viewed in his profile, a nasal piercing. Thus his profile name "Bull Ring". He was even taller in person, well over six foot tall. As he marched up to the porch, he exuded a confidence and could be intimidating to many as he approached. His muscles flexing – could probably snap me in two like a dried-out breadstick. But, I knew his willingness to serve.

He approached the porch, with head bowed.

"Sir, may I lick your boot, Sir?"

"Approach, boy."

He ascended the steps and prostrated himself in front of me.

"Sir, may I touch your boots, Sir?"

I gave him permission to do so, and he slowly began fondling the toes and heels of my boots.

He began a soft moaning.

"Sir," he began with his face close to the toe of the left boot, "permission to worship your left boot, Sir."

I once again gave him permission and he began a slow tongue massage of the boot. I could feel his tongue through the toe of the heavy Wesco. It was a slow and sensuous massage. My cock rose quickly in its Leather cod.

The boy never looked up, never made eye contact.

His head remained lowered as he requested permission to lick the right boot.

"Permission granted, boy."

A similar, prolonged tongue massage of the right boot ensued.

My cock was pulsating with manjuices as I viewed this handsome boy, the muscles in his arms and back flexing as he continued to lay in front of me.

As he began licking the shaft of the boot, I realized that this could take some time. Fine and good for him, he was getting off on the boot worship, but this Daddy wanted to be satisfied.

I pulled my flogger off my D ring. I began flogging his muscular back.

"Faster, boy."

He responded by taking longer strokes with his tongue, up to the knee. His fingers wrapped around the calf of the boot in an iron grip. Beads of sweat began to appear on his forehead.

"Boy, I want you to take off your boots and pants – service me buck naked." The boy reluctantly stopped his boot-worshipping, although he showed no hesitation in shedding his clothes. I quickly viewed a healthy cock and balls. His cock's head was pierced with a PA. Yet another reason for his nickname. And he lived up to the name – his handsome nutsac had been stretched on more than one occasion, his bullballs hung low.

"Back down on the floor, boy." He dropped. "Continue the boot worship."

I have to admit that I wanted to see his ass flexing, his cock and balls hanging between his muscular thighs. His arm muscles flexing. "Damn," I thought, "every Daddy should have a boy like this one."

As he began licking the thigh of the right boot, my cock was telling me it wanted a piece of the action.

With my gloved hand, I hooked my index finger in the bullring in the boy's nose. I pulled his head toward mine.

"Your LeatherMaster's cock needs some attention, Bull Ring."

With his head lowered, he simply responded, "Sir, Yes, Sir! It would be my immense pleasure."

His tongue began a slow exploration of the studded cod's surface. It flicked in among the studs, moistening the black Leather. The boy placed his arms behind his back. His shoulder and chest muscles flexed as he leaned toward my crotch.

When he had covered the surface of the cod with his tongue, he meekly said, "Sir, permission to unsnap your codpiece, Sir."

"Permission granted, boy."

He unsnapped it with his teeth. My juiced-up cock looked like a reversed pendulum as it was released, swinging back and forth as if celebrating its new-found freedom. The boy soon captured my cock in his mouth – swallowing the whole shaft. The nosering gently rubbed against my shaft as he swabbed my cock with that bootlicking mouth of his.

I knew I would not be able to control my cum release for too long. I was already horned up. A handsome boy servicing me. I began a slow pumping as he accommodated the rhythm of my cock pumping. Back and forth, thrusting.

My cock was coated by that boy's boot worshipping tongue. I once again pulled his head toward my cock, hooking my finger in the bullring inserted in his nose.

Pretty soon, the boy's head was buried in my crotch – his mouth vacuuming my overexcited cock.

The thrusting intensified. The vacuuming intensified. The boy's hands were still in back, resting on the small of his back. As I viewed his muscular body, I saw his ass muscles flexing. Anticipating what we would do next, I shot. Coating that bootsucking throat of his with a layer of cum. "Fuck!," I thought as a sigh escaped from my mouth. I pressed his head into my crotch with one hand and flogged his back and beautiful ass with the flogger in the other hand.

The boy continued to lick my cock until the cum juice was replaced with his saliva.

"Come with me, boy."

I marched down the steps of the porch and then down the steps to my dungeon.

"In, boy," I ordered, "On the table, boy. Face up." I placed a Leather pillow under his head. My workover table was not long enough to accommodate this boy. His legs hung off the end. We would have to take care of that situation. A series of rings were imbedded in the ceiling for such matters. I quickly put ankle restraints on each of his meaty legs and hoisted his feet toward the ceiling. His arms were fastened in a similar manner.

"Ah, yes, one more restraint." I quickly wrapped bondage rope around the base of his balls and cock, threaded it through that handy PA piercing, and ran the rope through yet another ring in the ceiling. Snake bite suckers on those handsome tits. It was a pleasure to work over this boy. Flogging, paddling, slapping. The first several rotations of floggings did not elicit a response – after all, he was very muscular. Just felt like a delicious warming of the skin, I surmised. As I intensified the rotations, he began to flinch. His head would occasionally roll from side to side. A soft moan. A flexing of the fingers. I knew I had struck a responsive chord. And his cock was a good barometer – it stayed firm and hard, being held aloft, in part, by its ring.

I stroked his cock and squeezed his balls, edging him toward climax. I sternly warned him that he would not cum until I told him to. I pumped up his nips with the snake bites. Pulling them off, his nips had swollen to the size of my thumb.

I worked on them with my gloved hands. Pinching, squeezing, rubbing. His cock was becoming harder and harder, I stroked his cock, pulled on those big bullballs. I was distracted, however. My mind kept flashing to that handsome ass of the captive boy. I wanted to work it over, explore it, satisfy my desires. Edging him toward climax, I abruptly stopped the titwork and cockplay. The boy moaned, pleading with his eyes for me to continue.

Instead, I raised the boy's feet until they were spread further apart and closer to the ceiling. As he attempted to reposition himself to a more comfortable position, my eyes kept looking at his handsome ass-flexing, tightening, revealing a hole worthy of exploration.

I wanted that muscular ass to play with. As I continued the flogging rotations, I began paddling it, slapping it, separating the cheeks, playfully sticking a finger or two in the crevice. The boy's ass muscles flexed, tightening, loosening. As I inserted two than three fingers, the boy began moaning.

I snapped on a latex glove and lubed it up. Time to go prospecting in a mineshaft.

I eased my fist up that boy's ass. The muscular contractions at first resisted the invasion, but as I talked the boy through it, his ass relaxed and my fist slid easily into place. My cock was fully aroused, its head appearing above the Leathered cod. I know what it wanted!

It was a pleasure having my fist up the boy's ass, but my cock always asserted itself when it came to man-to-boy sex. I withdrew my fist.

Dragging a crate over to the table, I stood on the makeshift platform, bringing my horny cock level to the boy's rear entrance. I lubed it up and slid it into the boy's hole.

"Oh, fuck," I thought, "this feels so good." His asscheeks expanded and contracted, encircling my cock's shaft, squeezing on it, pulling the cumjuices toward the piss slit.

"Fuck!" I thought, as I gyrated back and forth, my cock sliding in it a little further with each pumping. I tried to slow the process down, it felt so damned good. But that boy's ass just kept squeezing on my cock, willing my manjuices up his hole. Felt like the expert cock-sucking he had given me.

I tried to control it – mind over matter – but to no avail. In short order, I shot a load of cum up that boy's ass – and it felt delicious.

After I pulled out, I presented my cock to the boy's mouth for a swabbing. This boy was definitely a keeper.

I unmanacled him and led him to the porch. We stood with my Leather pressing against his naked body. I had to look up in order to catch his eyes. He lowered his head.

"Continue servicing my boots, boy, but, uh… start over at the toe." I wanted this boot worship and cock pleasuring to go on for a long time. One index finger encircled the bullring in his dick's head and one index finger encircled the bullring in his nose as I got right in his face, making sure to make eye contact. "And, boy… don't fuck up this time or we might have to have another session in the dungeon."

"Yes, Sir, i will do my best, Sir, but i'm only an apprentice bootlicker, Sir. i might not please Sir. i may have to be punished, Sir."

"All right – enough, son," as I slapped him lightly on the cheek and then pulled on both the rings.

I settled back in my chair and lighted a cigar. Spreading my legs, I motioned for him to prostrate himself on the floor.

The boot servicing began again.

LEATHERMAN CONSTRUCTION COMPANY

The Leatherman sat at his desk filling out work orders for the next day. Paperwork had become more and more of his duties as President of his own construction company. He had worked as a construction worker for a number of years, always for someone else. However, when the opportunity had presented itself, he had been able to purchase a small company outside the San Francisco Bay area. Under his guidance, the company had grown and he was very proud of the results. He was also proud of his Leather and founded the company based on his Leatherhood.

"Excuse me, Sir..." a boy's voice said.

"Just a minute, son..." and he raised his hand to indicate one minute. He continued to complete the work order and looked up.

A young man, approximately twenty-five years old, stood before him.

"What can I do for you, son?"

"I'd like to work for you."

"Have a seat, son" and the man continued to write for a few moments while mulling over the looks of the boy. The boy was slender, but that probably meant he was wiry, a swimmer's build.

"Okay, son, what experience do you have in the construction field?" The Leatherman eyed the boy while listening to the boy's response.

"Well, Sir, I grew up on a farm and helped my dad with all the duties – harvesting corn, running the tractor, that kind of stuff... I'm in pretty good shape, I work out with weights. One of your guys, Tom, told me about your company."

"Tom is an excellent worker; I don't think he would suggest you come here if he didn't think you could work with my crew...

What's your name, son?"

The boy answered "Frank", but it was obvious that he was distracted as he sat in front of the desk, absorbing every detail of the man behind the desk. He was a big muscled man and his tee shirt stretched across his muscular chest. The man wore black Leather wrist bands and tight-fitting black Leather gloves. The boy could see the waistband of black Leather pants.

The Leatherman took several drags on his big, black cigar, about the size of the boy's cock, he surmised.

The Leatherman outlined details of work duties, salary, vacation, and the requirements to work for his company. The boy nodded in agreement to every thing he heard.

"I'll start you tomorrow," said the Leatherman, as he handed the boy paperwork to fill out. "Come with me." As the man stood up, the boy's eyes immediately were focused on the Leatherman's codpiece which was a studded Leather codpiece. His eyes worshipped the heavy black construction boots on the man's feet. The man took the boy to the supply room, where he outfitted the boy with items required for his uniform. The man massaged his codpiece the entire time and the boy was easily distracted by the man's manipulation of his manmound. The man knew that he was exciting the boy and asked, "Any problems, son?"

"No, Sir, no problems at all," the boy responded enthusiastically. The boy grinned. The boy had passed the preliminary test by worshipping the man with his eyes, worship by other parts of his body would come later.

The Leatherman shook the boy's hand and gruffly announced, "Report here first thing in the morning, we start at 7:15 AM. No late shit – I don't care how long you stay in the bars but you report to me at 7:15."

"Yes, Sir." The boy exited. He avoided the bars that night and was back at work by 7 AM.

The Leatherman always held a meeting of the boys first thing in the morning to discuss the work orders. He had four concurrent projects and he liked to learn details of the progress made and any problems that arose. The Leatherman sat at the front of the room. He wore his black Leather harness, Leather armbands, his black Leather codpiece pants, and black construction boots. The boys filtered in. Each wore black Leather shorts, heavy black Leather workgloves, tool belts, and construction boots. A number of them wore tee shirts, but they would soon be discarded as the sun rose in the sky. The shed tee shirts would reveal nipple rings and tattoos. Each wore a black construction helmet with the company's name emblazoned on it.

"Good morning, boys. Looking at you makes me proud to be President of this company. Let's hear the progress on the remodeling of the playroom at the Musselman-Hill house." Tom and Jim were Leatherbuddies of the Leatherman and were having their playroom suite redesigned to include some new toys with separate units for the play parties they hosted. The Leatherbuddies liked to work one boy over at a time without interference from outside distractions.

Tony was site manager and reported, "All the units are now constructed. Each unit is now fully soundproofed. The walls are all lined with black Leather. We are installing the shackles, the racks and the slings today through Friday. We should have the project finished by next week. The room is beautiful. Mr. Musselman and Mr. Hill have been very pleased with all they have seen. They have invited us to their first play party…" Everyone laughed including the Leatherman.

"No doubt…" the Leatherman added, "Enter at your own risk, huh? Make sure all of us get an invitation to that party, Tony, don't keep it to yourself," Tony laughed easily, and agreed to that condition. The Leatherman knew that Tom and Jim were good men, upholding their Leather pride and would show everyone a good time.

"Okay, good. Tony, thank you. David, you are remodeling the private office suite of Mr. Thomas. Any problems?"

David reported that all was going according to schedule. Mr. Thomas' office included his photographic studio where he photographed Leathermen for portraiture as well as S&M scenes. Thomas did beautiful work. The Leatherman had several photographs taken by Thomas on his office walls. In fact, he had participated in several of the S&M shoots. The other two site managers, Joe and T.J., finished their respective reports. "T.J., I'm going to assign you our new worker, Frank." The Leatherman introduced Frank, who was seated near the back of the room. He stood up nervously, but was greeted by a resounding welcome. He proudly wore the Construction Company's tee shirt and his laced-up Leather shorts given to him the day before.

The details continued with a final reminder from the Leatherman. "I want you all to keep your Leather shined, and that includes your boots… I can see a few that haven't been shined lately." The boys quickly looked down to see if they were the transgressors. "Marcus, stay behind for a few minutes…" the Leatherman ordered, before dismissing the workers. The Leatherman watched the black-Leathered asses file out of the room.

Marcus was a dark-haired boy, with a big bushy mustache and lots of body hair. He was hunky and he knew it.

After the boys had left, the Leatherman escorted Marcus to his office. "Sit down, son," the Leatherman commanded.

Marcus eyed him squarely and said, "What did I do wrong?" He was a hard-worker and felt singled out.

"Nothing, son, you haven't done anything wrong. I call my boys in on occasion just to thank them for a job well-done. You are a good worker and I am really glad to have you working for me. Joe has given me excellent reports about your work on the project."

Marcus relaxed. "How about a cigar, son?" With that the Leatherman offered a hefty black cigar from the humidor on his desk. He lit the cigar for Marcus.

"I'm proud of you, Marcus, because I know you had a rough life before you came to me… fill me in."

The two talked for twenty minutes and by the end of the session, Marcus was kneeling before the Leatherman, with the Leatherman's cock in his mouth. The Leatherman reached down to tweak the boy's nipples with his black Leathered glove hands. He pulled the boy's mouth to his own. The two engaged in a tonguing and then the boy returned to sucking the man off. The Leatherman moaned with pleasure – he had heard from his workers that Marcus was a good cocksucker. "I just had to find out for myself," he thought to himself as he exploded in the boy's throat.

"Good work, son. I'm going to hand you the next project as site manager. Keep up the good work." He slapped the grateful boy on his ass and sent him on to his work site.

The Leatherman continued for about an hour on paperwork, telephone calls, emails, and all the business shit. He climbed aboard his Harley and visited each of the worksites. All the men were hard at work, predictably with their shirts off, their handsome chests rippling with muscles underneath the morning sun.

The Leatherman stood back. The boys were a wonderful group of young men – reliable, hardworking, and unfortunately, playful. More than once, he had to discipline a boy for his lusty ventures on company time. He carried a small paddle with him, tucked into the top of his boot, just to keep the boys in line.

Of course, the discipline rarely worked, they enjoyed it too much. Daddy's paddle was a reward, not a deterrent. "Still in all, they work most of the time…and I get a decent day's work out of them."

The Leatherman continued to inspect the sites – adding a suggestion here and there. At the last site, an expansion of a Leather store on Castro street, he placed his Leather hat aside, put on a construction helmet, and pitched in alongside his workers. Soon sweat glistened on his chest and back. He could feel the sweat trickling down his waistband and down his asscheeks. He wiped the sweat from his forehead and drunk in the manly smell of sweat and warmed Leather. His thoughts were soon focused on the new boy, Frank. Frank worked without stopping, pausing only momentarily to wipe the sweat from his forehead. Frank seemed to be fitting in well, with good-natured teasing and slapping of asses punctuating the work crew's dedication to finishing the project and finishing it well. The Leatherman approached Frank and slapped him on the ass.

"How's it going, son?"

"Just fine, Sir… the guys are great…"

"Come with me, son." He waved momentarily to T.J., indicating Frank was going with him. They approached the worksite shed on the adjacent parking lot.

"In, boy."

Frank marched into the worksite shed, only to view a rack with shackles.

Frank's jaw dropped, but before he knew what was happening, the Daddy had strapped his wrists to the shackles, face toward the wall.

"Have… I done something wrong?"

"No, son, you've done everything right. This is just a little pleasure for the lunchtime hour."

With that the Daddy pulled the paddle from his boot, and began smacking the young boy's ass. It was obvious that the boy had never experienced anything like this before, but a shy smile on his face indicated that he was proud that he had been singled out, enjoying being worked over by his new boss.

As the boy peered over his shoulder, he was entranced by the muscular Daddy who was in his Leathers and wore a construction helmet.

The man pulled the boy's Leather shorts down roughly and soon Leather was tanning the ass of the new construction worker. The other fellows kept working outside, because they all knew what was transpiring inside the shed. They had all experienced, and relished, the workout.

The paddling intensified and then abruptly stopped.

The Leatherman repositioned the boy and soon a flogger was flogging the boy's sensitive cock and balls. The cock was indeed similar to the cigar clenched between the man's teeth. The boy's balls hung low.

The Daddy talked to the boy the entire time he was flogging or paddling him. He talked him through the session and the boy was smiling more broadly with each lash. His cock had responded and was stiff and proud.

The man abruptly stopped and released the boy from the shackles. "Show your gratitude, son."

The boy fell to his knees and began licking the Leatherman's dusty construction boots. The man's cock hardened inside his codpiece.

The man guided the boy's hands to the codpiece and the boy began massaging his Daddy's dick inside the cod. When instructed, he pulled the codpiece off and began sucking his newly-found Daddy's dick. The man's cock eased down the boy's throat and soon shot a load of jism down the boy's willing throat.

The man stroked the boy's head with his black Leather gloved hands and pulled him toward him. The boy and the man kissed long and hard while the man manipulated the boy's cock. It soon exploded on the Leatherman's pants.

"I'm sorry, Sir, I didn't mean to…"

"It's all right, son, first time workers are bound to make a few mistakes…," as he pushed the boy's face into the fresh cum. The boy licked up his own cum.

The Leatherman pulled the boy's head back up, so that the boy was looking squarely into the face of his new boss.

"After all, son, you are still under construction as one of my boys…"

The boy grinned, the Leatherman laughed, they stuck their respective cocks back into place and both went back to work.

IN A FOG

The yellowish orange of a match's flame lit the darkened river bank. A brief flare and then a puff of smoke as the flame caught to the end of the Leatherman's long, black cigar. Every night the Leatherman set out for a late night walk, and this night was no exception. He enjoyed the pleasure of a good, strong cigar after dinner or after sex. This particular night was his after-dinner pleasure.

"No sex," he thought, with horny thoughts swirling around underneath his Leather hat. He walked to his favorite spot, a secluded part of the woods, which reached along the Susquehanna River. He enjoyed watching the rippling of the water underneath the moonlight. The moonlight created striated patterns on the surface of the water. The stars punctuated the surface with pin dots of light. Tonight was a typical autumn in Pennsylvania. The nights were pretty chilly, and the man had layered himself in longjohns, denim, and Leather. He walked down the path which he had himself created by repeat occasions. The cigar was heady and the man drew on it deeply. He closed his eyes momentarily as he drew several more puffs.

He found his favored spot – a tree trunk, which had partially fallen, creating a natural seat. He swung his right leg over the log and settled into place, his Leathered back resting against the upper portion of the log. He stroked his hardened cock through the denim. The water rippled. An occasional leaf fell, joining many others on the heavily-carpeted forest floor.

Moon beams shafted down through the filtering of leaves, and one shaft of light caught the side zippers of the man's chaps. He began stroking the softened Leathers on his upper thighs with his hands which were encased in black Leather gauntlets.

"Ah, shit, man, there ain't nothing better than a man in his Leathers…"

A strong breeze picked up and the man shivered despite his layers of protective gear.

The man longed for a nice firm body to couple with and hell, to provide some warmth. It was damned-side chilly out here.

The Leatherman continued to stare out toward the river. His thoughts once again returned to his relationship with Clint. Clint had been the Leatherman's lover for three years. They had had such a good relationship. The Leatherman had introduced Clint to the pleasures of Leather & S&M. The Leatherman had moved to Pennsylvania to be nearer Clint. Clint owned a starkly beautiful stone farmhouse in rural Pennsylvania. At the time of their meeting, Clint had been looking for work. It was after an unsuccessful interview that Clint had been drowning his sorrows in the Leatherman's favorite bar in New Jersey when the Leatherman spotted him. The man was handsome, no doubt about it. He had pure white hair and the tightest white jeans. "Well," the Leatherman thought, "it's not Leather, but it sure as hell ain't bad." He sauntered over to the man, introduced himself, and asked the guy if he could buy him a drink. Their first conversation lasted three and a half hours. After that evening, they quickly became lovers, but it took the Leatherman some time to convince Clint that Leather was erotic and powerful. Clint, once he tried it out, had embraced it warmly. To be nearer Clint, the Leatherman had moved to Pennsylvania and was able to find work within a couple of weeks.

Clint was still unemployed eight months later when the Leatherman's job fell through. The men struggled financially for some time before Clint had called it quits, sold the stone farmhouse, and had moved in with his former lover. Now, the Leatherman was stuck in Pennsylvania with no job and no lover.

"Shit happens," he thought, as he brooded about the loss of Clint.

The Leatherman continued to stoke his cigar, while he absently rubbed his hardening denim-covered cock with his Leather gauntlet. Clouds were moving in slowly, obscuring the moon and starlight. A sturdy breeze continue to snatch leaves from almost-bare branches, sending them down in torrents onto the ground.

Now that Clint was out of the picture, the Leatherman was alone. There weren't many Leathermen in the little shitwater town to which he had moved. In fact, there was only one other guy into Leather that he knew about. The guy was married. His wife liked to watch and photograph the sessions that her husband participated in. And sure, there were plenty of bikers who raced through town in their cycle Leathers, but they weren't from the area, and they usually had a woman riding with them. The town's people were typically narrow-minded and uniformly stupid, and sure as hell didn't understand a man who walked around in full, black Leather. The Leatherman's only solace was to take long walks in the woods and hope and pray that another Leatherman would show his Leathered ass soon.

The Leatherman continued to sit on the log and smoke. His dick was nice and hard, despite the cold weather. As he watched the river, a heavy fog began rolling in, making steady progress down the Susquehanna. "Jesus," he thought, "it's so fucking erotic. It makes the landscape even more mysterious than it is." And it was true, everything was veiled in a shroud of pale white mist as the moon disappeared behind a bank of clouds. A brief wind stirred and the trees sent down a few of their remaining leaves to join the others which had fallen before.

The Leatherman gazed into the milky-white expanse. As he looked across the stretch of water, a single brightened light appeared. It moved in an arch, up and down, glowing brighter at times when it reached upward. After concentrating on the movement for a few moments, the Leatherman realized that it was a cigar being stoked. He stood up, and moved his cigar in a similar fashion. Soon, the cigar on the opposite shore was moving in rhythm to his own cigar.

The Leatherman yelled, "Hey, Buddy, cold enough for you?" and soon the echoed reply,

"Sure as frozen shit." was heard.

He moved down to the muddied shore, but still could not discern anything other than a vague shape.

A flash of light from a match and a lantern was lighted on the opposite shore. The figure sat the lantern at his feet. The Leatherman still could not see much, other than the figure was a man. He raised his hand in greeting, not knowing if the man on the other shore had better visibility than himself.

The lantern was picked up and held near the bottom of the man's face on the opposite shore. The Leatherman could see that the man was bearded, but still little else.

"Hey, Buddy, I got my boat here, if you'll stay there, I'll row across…"

"Sure thing, Buddy…" the Leatherman replied.

Splashing, followed by a brief curse, was heard. This was followed by a larger splash and more cursing.

The regular paddling of oars was finally heard and within a few minutes, the Leatherman could make out a seated figure in a small boat.

The Leatherman helped pull the boat up on the shore and helped the man out of the boat. For a minute, the Leatherman thought he was looking in a mirror. The dude was dressed in head-to-toe Leather.

"Hey, Buddy, thanks for pulling my boat up... well, hell, another Leatherman...in this fucking goddamned town? ...well, I'll be damned." the second Leatherman said.

"Shit, am I glad to see you...I'm Dick."

"Well, hell, Buddy, that's a damned appropriate name because I'm Peter."

The men both laughed easily.

Peter pulled out matches, but they had gotten soggy and so Dick presented him with a fresh cigar, lit from his own cigar.

"Shit, man, look at you, you're soaked from head to toe."

"Ah, hell, I missed my footing in this damned fog, fell right in..."

Dick gathered some fallen branches, bunches of the dried leaves, and soon, the men were enjoying the warmth of a fire. A stiffer autumn breeze began blowing and despite the fire, Peter began shivering uncontrollably.

"Sorry, man, I would have brought a blanket along if I'd thought I was gonna be camping tonight – I just came out for a smoke, I didn't expect to meet anybody."

"Well, I tell you, Buddy, if you could get closer to me, I'd sure appreciate it."

The first Leatherman didn't need another invitation for that activity.

The two men fell into an easy camaraderie. They talked about cycles, hunting, football, and as if by electrical impulse, sex. The first Leatherman, always proud of his sexuality, and horny for sex, announced his interest in S&M.

"Well, shit, Buddy, me too!" With that, he grabbed the first Leatherman's basket and began manipulating it. Pretty soon, the Leathermen were rolling round on the bank, alternately on top of one another. They tore at each other's crotches and asses like wild animals. Each was making grunting sounds. Nipples and ass cheeks were slapped, chewed on, and molested in any way they could think. Pretty soon, the 501s were opened, the longjohns unbuttoned, and two hard dicks were exploring as the fog continued to roll down the Susquehanna.

After sex, the men relaxed, huddling as near the fire as possible. The fog hid the nearby river, the clouds had totally obscured the moon and stars, and the Pennsylvania night was rapidly dropping toward freezing.

"Well, man, I guess I'd better haul ass...I'm still pretty damp. I gotta get some rest. I gotta go to work in the morning..." Peter stood up, and the two men embraced warmly. Each other knew another Leatherman in town now, and wasn't likely to forget how to contact each other. Peter strode down the bank. As he turned to raise his hand in greeting, he lost his footing in the river bank mud. "Aw, shit, not again...," as he tumbled into the water. His hands flailed forward, managing to grasp on the side of the boat.

"Hold on," Dick yelled, "let me help."

A few seconds later, his body landed beside Peter in the water. "Well, shit," Dick gasped, as he spouted a mouthful of the Susquehanna. Both men clung to the side of the boat. Peter eased himself over the edge of the boat and collapsed in the bottom. "Come on in, Buddy, there's room..."

Dick eased himself over the side, but slipped as he was climbing in, landing square on top of Peter. WHOMPF, as the two bodies slammed into one another.

"Well, hell, Buddy, I didn't know you liked me that much!"

"Shit, I was trying to retrieve your mangy ass from the water... Fuck, now I'm as wet as you are..."

The two men began laughing at their predicament. "Man, I knew I had wet dreams about Leathermen, but this wasn't quite what I thought they were all about..."

After laughing for a few seconds, both men realized that the boat was in motion. It had been loosened from its place on the bank and the two men were making a slow journey down the Susquehanna.

"Time to break out the old oars... where the hell did I put them?"

"Oh, no, man, you brought them onto shore, remember?"

For the fourth or fifth time that evening, cursing was heard on the Susquehanna.

"Well, man, what do we do now?"

"Well, man, we make the best of it..."

With that, Dick reached under Peter's jacket and gave the man's tits a hard twist. "I say we fuck in a canoe, how about you?"

Peter was already moaning from the pressure exerted on his tits by the soft Leather gauntlets. His dick hardened through his dampened Leather "Yeah, sounds like a pretty good idea, Kemozabe!"

The Leatherman controlled the situation. He nuzzled the man's face with his beard, nibbling the man's earlobes, and licked the man's lips. Soon his tongue was exploring the inner recesses of his man's mouth. The man's tongue responded in kind. With his left hand, Dick unbuttoned his companion's shirt, lifted his tee shirt and began rubbing and rolling the guy's left tit. The tit responded, becoming firm and hard.

With his right hand, Dick rubbed his gloved hand against the hardened basket of Leather. He could trace the cock's head and shaft through the Leather. The cock pulsed in response to his touch.

Peter was not idle. His left hand reached up and massaged Dick's chest. His right hand had a firm grip on Dick's basket. He alternately tugged at Dick's cock and then massaged the Leatherman's balls. The boat continued to drift down the Susquehanna. The fog swirled around the two lovers, obscuring their lovemaking from view.

Dick stopped rubbing Peter's left tit.

"Hey, don't stop, man it feels damned good…"

"Yeah, okay, man, just a minute…"

With his free hand, he reached in and pulled out his cigar case. The case was waterproof and his cigars remained dry.

"Let's have a cigar, huh?" With that he lighted the two, and handed his boy one. They dragged on their cigars as they continued to prod and pull on each other's cocks and tits.

The fog continued to intensify, and the boat was lost from view.

Dick began manipulating Peter's tits once again. They were hardened. Without warning, he took the lighted end of his cigar and applied it directly to his lover's right tit.

"AAWWW," screamed the second Leatherman, "SHIT! It feels so damned good."

"Take it like the Leatherman you are, man!" commanded Dick.

With that, he applied his cigar to the other tit. The bottom responded by wincing and rolling from side to side. The boat rocked precariously.

"Stop it, man, you're gonna dump us in the river, you shithead…"

Dick continued to alternate the cigar between left and right tit, encircling the nipple until all the hair around it was singed. He then pulled out his alligator tit clamps and put them on the aching nipples. The contrast of the burning ash and the cold metal caused Peter to cry out once again.

The pain was good, however, and Peter really enjoyed it. He reached up and caressed his master's chest. "Oh, yeah, man, don't stop now, man, it feels so fuckin' good…" He pulled on his master's nipples.

"All right, man," Dick said, "turn-about is fair play, burn my tits!"

The bottom applied his smoldering cigar to the man's left tit and then his right tit. Dick moaned with pleasure. He arched his back so that the mounds of tit flesh would push forward to be closer to the cigar. "GRRINNNDD it in, man. Yeah, man, that's it. Burn those nips, man! I want you to take every bit of fuckin' body hair off my body with your cigar, man. Yeah, man!"

The Leatherman writhed and moaned while the bottom performed his task. Both men had raging hard-ons from the activity.

"Now, man, I want you to take you cigar and trace the outline of my cock on my jeans," Dick commanded.

The hot ash of the cigar singed the denim fabric and soon the Leatherman's cock was seen in clear outline, throbbing up and down, fully extended.

After several minutes, the Leatherman knew he was going to shoot, and so he demanded that his bottom take the cock in his mouth. The man sat up in the boat, grasping on the Leatherman's hips for balance. He ripped the remainder of the blue jeans and then unbuttoned the longjohns. The Leatherman's dick, sensing freedom, arched forward. It rose toward the clouded heavens.

The bottom was now licking his lips in great anticipation of a suck feast.

His lips closed around the head of the cock and he began sucking with great pleasure. He held his cigar in his right hand. His right hand held the cigar near the base of the Leatherman's balls. They responded to the warmth of the cigar and became loose and pliable. Peter began massaging them with his left hand.

His mouth continued to suck up and down on the hardened cock. It filled Peter's mouth and he moaned with gratitude.

While his genitals were being serviced, the Leatherman continued to fire up his boy's tits with his lighted cigar. The tits were still clamped with the alligators, and the fired-up metal made the tits burn with sexual passion. With his free hand, the Leatherman tugged on the chain which connected the two clamps.

"Aah, yeah, son, that's right, I'm gonna burn those tits of yours…"

The Leatherman pulled on the chain repeatedly, yanking the tits further and further from his boy's chest. The tits were burned and aching, but were also burning and aching with pleasure.

Peter continued to manipulate Dick's hardened cock in his mouth – the cock throbbed with pleasure. Finally, after a suck that enveloped the whole cock to its base, the Leatherman's dick shot a load of cum down his newly-found boy's throat.

"AAAHHHH!" was heard along the banks of the Susquehanna, but anyone who happened to have heard it, only wondered if the Canada geese were heading south already.

Finally, the Leatherman reached down and grabbed his boy's genitalia with his gloved hands. He unbuttoned Peter's Levis only to find that the piss-slit was already filled with pre-cum, and it only took two minutes for Peter to shoot.

"Aaah, shit, man, that was fucking good…"

The boat continued to float down the Susquehanna, Somewhat aimlessly. The two Leathered men relaxed in one another's embrace and continued to suck on their cigars. The heat of their sexual frenzy had kept them warm, but the temperature had dropped steadily since their departure from the warmth of the fire. As they looked from the boat, they could see nothing but fog. The fog had obscured all landmarks.

"Shit, man, where the fuck are we?" Peter asked.

The Leatherman pulled his newly-found boy closer to him.

"We're on the mighty Susquehanna, where anything is possible. Some men have described the river as the most beautiful in the country. Also one of the most mysterious – she swallows up her secrets and doesn't reveal them."

The fog swirled around his head, obscuring the features of his boy.

The next morning, Charlie Phillips went down to the bank to check his muskrat traps. Odd, he thought, there was a boat which had banked on a small mudflat. He picked his way carefully down to it. The boat was empty.

On a night when the fog reaches up and obscures the moonlight and shrouds the river in mystery, the two Leathermen still smoke their cigars and fuck each other in a boat on the Susquehanna. Lest you think this is a legend of the Susquehanna, be assured that the men are very much alive. As was their luck that evening, the boat hit a rock and the men had to swim to shore. Cursing was once again heard along the banks of the Susquehanna.

NIGHTSTICK

The Leatherman and his boy were relaxing on the back porch of the Leatherman's house. The Leatherman clenched a long, black cigar between his teeth and the boy's shaven head between his muscular legs. The boy, clad only in a black Leather jockstrap, was servicing the man's cock, greedily slurping the juiced up tool with his eager slave lips. The night was a balmy summer night in Pennsylvania and all was right with the world. Or so, it seemed.

The boy would occasionally come up for air, but his head would be roughly pushed back down as soon as the Leatherman felt the boy should return to his duties.

"You like my cock, don't you, boy?"

The boy shook his head and continued his duties.

The Leatherman twisted his own nipples with his gloved hands. The pain was delicious. When the boy had satisfied Daddy's cock needs, the boy would turn his attentions to the man's tits.

The silence of the night was suddenly deafened with the roar of two motorcycles – Harleys by the sound of it.

Pretty soon, the cycles roared into the long driveway which separated the man's property from the rest of the world. The Leatherman instinctively knew who it was, but the boy was startled and stopped his servicing and started to stand. He was pushed back down to his knees.

"I didn't tell you to get up, asshole…"

"Yes, Sir," the boy mumbled as he continued his tonguing of the shaft of the man's cock.

Moments later, two cycles pulled into the yard. The boy instinctively turned around only to witness two cops.

"Oh, Shit, Sir… we've been caught."

He was slapped across the face and told to continue.

"I'll take care of this," the Leatherman confidently said, "you just continue what you're doing."

The two cops approached the porch. They were dressed in tan uniforms and knee-high boots, spit-shined to perfection.

"Sir," the younger of the two cops addressed the Leatherman, momentarily startled to notice a young, mostly naked boy, sucking on the man's privates, "we are here…"

"Yeah, what the fuck do you want, you piece of shit."

The other cop approached the porch, "We are here, Sir, on official business."

"Oh, you are? Well, fuck you too."

With that the two cops pulled out their nightsticks and started up the steps.

The boy was nervously eyeing them, and had ceased the performance of his duties.

The Daddy pulled a paddle off the arm of the chair and spanked the boy's ass several times. "You continue, you fuck-up."

Despite the warning, the boy continued to stare at the cops and began trembling, "Sir, I've never been in any trouble with the law…"

"Relax, boy, now get back to your duties." He returned his attention to the cops who brandished the nightsticks as they cautiously approached the Leatherman and boy.

"What can I do for you, boys?"

"Sir, as we said we are on official duty," one of the cops said, ignoring the reference to them being called 'boys'.

With that, the Leatherman pushed the boy away and stood to his full-length. He was magnificent in full head-to-toe Leather.

"You fuckers are on my property…"

"We know, Sir… we only have one thing to tell you."

"What's that?"

"How are you, Sir?" and with that they broke into broad, shit-eating grins.

The men embraced.

"What's going on?" the boy asked, despite the fact that he might be whipped again.

"These are two of Daddy's boys, Ryan and Mark. They're not cops – they're just Leathermen in the making. Take a look at their uniforms, boy, the uniforms are Leather."

It was true – the tan shirts and ass-tight pants were tan Leather, Blue Leather stripes ran down the legs until disappearing into the tops of their Dehners.

The Leather cops sat down in the adjoining chairs and the man sent the boy in to the house to make drinks and bring a selection of cigars.

"Who's this cute little boy?" Ryan asked.

"My new boy, Hal, he's been with me for about three months and he's a fast learner."

When the boy returned, all three men sat with their long, delicious cocks hanging out of their pants. Each fondled his respective cock and balls as the boy served the drinks. The boy had punched the cigars, kneeling in front of each man to light a precious Cuban from his Leatherdaddy's private stock.

The men stoked their cigars as the boy knelt in turn before each one and sucked their hardened rods.

The boy had never experienced such ecstasy, serving not only his Master's cock, but being allowed to service the dicks of two other hot men.

The Leatherman removed his jacket to reveal his considerable pecs, a harness and nipple rings. Soon the other two followed suit and the boy had his mouth filled with dicks, balls, or mantits for the next hour. The men conversed while Hal performed his slave duties.

Daddy would occasionally scold him, or he would be smacked by one of the three men. His dick hardened each time.

Ryan stood up and moved behind the boy. Without warning, he took his nightstick and shoved the tip of the nightstick up the unsuspecting boy's ass.

The boy winced in pain and the three men laughed.

He recovered quickly and begged his newly-found cop Daddy to do it again, if he so desired.

Ryan just laughed, but Mark quickly complied with his nightstick.

"Daddy, Sir," Mark requested, "we'd like to work your boy over for you."

The Daddy nodded his consent and the boy was quickly handcuffed with a pair of handcuffs pulled off the back of Ryan's fully-stocked Sam Browne belt.

The two Leathercops led the boy to the Leatherman's well-stocked playroom and the three men lifted him into place in the black Leather sling.

They quickly manacled the boy into place so that he could not move very much. The boy was placed face down, his cute ripe ass pointing fuckward.

The men exited, leaving Hal to ponder his fate. They returned to the porch.

They sat on the porch and continued pulling on their cocks, one another's, and smoking their aromatic cigars.

They reminisced about the former days when each boy in turn had been the Leatherdaddy's boy. They had grown into handsome Leathermen, but had never forgotten their Leatherdaddy, whom they loved and respected. They talked about their recent adventures and misadventures. After a good thirty minutes, they returned to the playroom. Hal lay calmly, although he did crane his neck nervously toward them as they stomped into the playroom with their big, handsome Leather boots. Daddy stood to the left of the boy, while Ryan stood near his feet, and Mark assumed the position opposite the Leatherman. The Leatherman had a well-stocked playroom and so, the cops had left their play items on their cycles.

Each man paddled Hal's ass from the positions where they stood – east, south, and west.

The boy could feel his cock hardening with each rotation. His ass flesh felt tenderized, but he was enjoying the sensational feeling.

A can of lube made its appearance, as each man greased up a Leathered hand. Hal knew what that meant, and he squeezed his eyes shut as he anticipated a fist up his ass.

The Leatherdaddy was the first to fist him and Hal's head jerked back as the fist inched up his rectum. Daddy's fisting was powerful and Hal hoped it wouldn't stop. The fisting seemed to go on forever as the Daddy massaged and slapped the boy's asscheeks with his other gloved hand. The cops simply observed. However, when the Daddy's fist was withdrawn, they were quick to take over. Ryan's fist was the next insertion while Mark lashed the boy's tender asscheeks with a flogger. When Ryan's fist was finally withdrawn, Mark shoved the end of his nightstick up the boy's ass. In quick succession, two more nightsticks were attempting to enjoy their brother of abuse up the same hole.

"His hole isn't big enough..." Mark observed.

"It will be in time, our Leatherdaddy will make sure of that," Ryan remarked and they laughed, apparently from collective memories of sore asses.

A hand roughly pulled Hal's cock from beneath his belly and began squeezing it. Another hand began pulling on his balls and yet another hand was flogging Hal's bare back.

The delicious abuse continued as the sun sunk below the horizon. The boy's ass, dick, back, and balls were hurting, but he didn't mind it a bit.

All three Leathermen agreed that Hal was a good boyslave.

"I'm just troubled by one thing, Sir..." Mark suggested.

"Ummm, what's that?" the Leatherdaddy questioned as he continued to flog his boy's ass.

"His nightstick potential."

"Son," the Leatherdaddy, "that's my uncharted territory; I'll take care of it."

"Yes, Sir."

The Daddy greased up his own manrod, a healthy substitute for the wooden nightstick which was casually laid on the work table.

He crawled on top of the boy and his dick was soon inserted in the boy's willing hole. The boy groaned as his Daddy's pole pounded his hole with a frenzied pumping. The Leatherman prolonged the pleasurable experience, but finally climaxed in the boy's butt. His manrod was quickly replaced by Ryan's dick, which creamed in short order. Finally, Mark's cock pumped his jism into the willing boy's hole.

The men flipped the boy over in the sling, revealing a healthy hard-on.

"Please, Daddies, may I cum, please, Sirs?"

The two cops looked to their Leatherdaddy who responded "Yes, but only when I tell you to, boy."

The three men helped the boy along by alternately stroking the boy's cock, working on his boytits, and inserting gloved fingers in his mouth.

After what seemed an eternity to the boy, he received the command to shoot.

He shot a geyser of cum and the men were quick to smear it on his face and chest. He was not allowed to taste his own cum.

Instead, he was taken out of the sling and placed on his knees on the floor.

The men manipulated their cocks to hardness and then proceeded to piss on the boy. He lapped up the piss that landed on his mouth and chin.

"Thank you, Daddies…"

"boy," the Leatherdaddy said, "my two sons have decided to spend a couple of days here… this was Session One. Are you up for the rest of the sessions, boy?"

Not wanting Session One to end, the boy was not sure how many more sessions there would be, but he only had to think momentarily before answering enthusiastically, "Yes, Sir."

The Leatherdaddy and his three boys returned to the porch, where they enjoyed the rest of their cigars and freshly-poured drinks. Daddy and his boycops rested their booted feet on Hal's back. He proved to be a very willing coffee table. He also served as a willing ashtray as they flicked the cigar ashes into his receptive mouth. The boy relished both – the momentary sting of the hot ash and the Leathermen's boots pressing into his flesh. When told, he gladly polished all three sets of kneehigh boots with his slaveboy's tongue.

At the end of the three day session, the boy was very accommodating to three men's nightsticks. It would be fantasy to think the boy could take three nightsticks up his ass, two was his limit. The third was inserted in his willing mouth – he sucked on it as if it were the tastiest cock. The tastiest cocks replaced it in quick succession.

ON THE RIGHT TRACK

The Leatherman led the slaveboy deep into the woods. He was following an abandoned railroad track which had cut through the Pennsylvania woods in the nineteenth century. The tracks had long since been abandoned for more modern modes of transportation. The tracks were overgrown and some of the ties had rotted away. Nature had begun to reclaim the manmade features that had disturbed the deep, wooded forest.

The Leatherman knew his way. He had taken other boys to this chosen, secluded spot. The boy carried the bondage and torture equipment necessary for a play session in a black Leather bag. The boy was hooded and blindfolded, with a buttplug in his mouth. The boy wore boots, a jockstrap and a collar with pinpricks – all he would need until they got to the Leatherman's chosen destination. The collar was attached to a leash, gripped firmly in the Leatherman's gloved hand. The Leatherman wore an executioner's hood and full Leather. High boots. A long, black cigar jutted forth from his Leather-covered jaw.

If the boy seemed to lag, several sharp pulls on the leash coaxed him forward, grinding pinpricks into the soft flesh of the boy's neck.

It was approximately half an hour before they reached their destination.

"Drop the bag here, slave," he ordered. The slave complied.

The Leatherman reached into the bag and retrieved a bottle of water. He unscrewed the cap on the bottle of water and pressed it between the slave's lips. The slave gulped greedily.

"That won't be the only liquid refreshment you'll receive, boy." the Leatherman stated as he tilted the bottle backward.

When he felt the slave had received enough water, he hastily closed the bottle and began pulling out his necessary supplies. The only sounds that were heard was birdsong throughout the trees.

The Leatherman pulled out four lengths of black bondage rope. He placed several floggers on the D ring of his pants.

He eased the slave down across the railroad tracks, laying the boy on his back. He kicked the boy's feet apart, spreadeagling them. The boy's arms were also spreadeagled. Each appendage was secured to a part of the railroad track. The boy's chest was heaving.

"Settle down, slave!" the Leatherman yelled, kicking the boy in the ribcage.

The slave whimpered, but said nothing. The buttplug in his mouth prevented speech.

The Leatherman stood over his slave. He placed his booted feet underneath each asscheek.

The Leatherman began massaging his already-excited cock still in its Leather cod.

He puffed on his cigar, viewing the secluded location. "Perfect location for a man to work over his slave," the Leatherman said out loud, for his own benefit and for the benefit of the boy. Although the boy's hearing was impaired by the tight black Leather hood, he knew the slave could still hear his directions and orders.

The Leatherman reached into the Leather bag and extracted a pair of titclamps. He squatted, attaching the nip clamps to the slave's virgin tits.

The boy's head shook from side to side as the pressure of the clamps exerted themselves on his nips.

For good measure, the Leatherman yanked on the chain. The slave let out a muffled scream. The Leatherman yanked them several times more, making sure they were firmly attached.

The Leatherman reached into the bag once more and pulled out a cockring with weights attached. It soon encircled the boy's cock and balls. Even though not hanging straight down, the weights exerted pressure on the boy's equipment. The boy once again rolled his head from side to side, muttering something. The Leatherman kicked the boy's ass with his steel-toed boots, "Shut the fuck up, slave." The boy stopped his whining but continued to roll his head from side to side.

The Leatherman took several long drags on his cigar and then the flogging began.

The only sounds in the woods now was the repeated lashing of Leather straps against slaveflesh. Again and again, as the straps caught the ribcage and tits of the slave. The slave pulled against his restraints, but it was to no avail. He would not loosen them, the Leatherman was an excellent ropesman.

The Leatherman continued to strap the slave, attempting to redden every inch of the slave's floggable body. He had a boyish body. Small tits which the Leatherman wished to enlarge through repeated use. The slave's dick, of decent size, was stretched as were the boy's taut balls. The slave's body reddened nicely. Lash marks were apparent. The boy cried out whenever the flogger hit the titclamp chain, pulling on it and increasing the pressure on the slave's nips. Shoulders, upper chest, and ribcage were flogged, with an occasional flick of the flogger to the boy's cock and balls just to keep the boy under his sadistic control.

The Leatherman's dick had hardened nicely. He massaged it in its Leather enclosure in between floggings.

As the session continued, the Leatherman's mancock was pulsing with the excitement of flogging the slavemeat.

Sensing that he could not hold his juices any longer, the Leatherman unsnapped his cod and rubbed the veined shaft with his gloved hand. A spray of jism issued forth, landing on the boy's torso. Several more spurts of cum dripped out of the man's cock and landed squarely on the boy's abused body.

He let the cum dry on the boy's torso before resuming the flogging. The Leatherman's cock now swung freely. It hardened quickly from the continued floggings, proudly announcing that it was the mancock of a sadistic LeatherMaster. After another long session of flogging, the Leatherman felt the need to relieve himself and that's what he did – spraying the boy from head to toe with his golden shower. The boy was moaning.

"I told you to shut the fuck up, slave!" the Leatherman commanded, as he kicked the boy's ass once more.

"Time to turn you over, slave," the Leatherman said as he repositioned the boy on his stomach. The slave showed no resistance as he was tied into place once more.

"Ah, look at that fucking hot ass." the Leatherman said to himself, a smile appearing on his handsome face.

With that, a fresh barrage of beatings on the boy's back and ass ensued. With each strike, the Leatherman seemed to increase the intensity. The back was soon crisscrossed with the marks left by the tails of the flogger.

The Leatherman stood back to admire his handiwork. The boy's back was a tribute to his status as a LeatherSadist. During the session, the boy began moaning, even though he had been told repeatedly to remain silent. A booted foot was planted firmly on the small of the boy's back as the Leatherman leaned down and hissed, "You'll moan even more when you feel my next toy, slaveboy."

Kneeling in between the boy's spread legs, the Leatherman lubed up his cock with a gob of spit. His Leatherspade dug deep into the boy's hole. At first, the boy squeezed his ass shut and was objecting to the invasion in muffled tones.

As the Leatherman guided his cock further into the boy's hole, he pulled up the boy's head by the Leather hood, and whispered hoarsely, "You are my fuckslave, now get used to it." The Leatherman stretched his Leather-covered arms over the boy's. He occasionally reached underneath to tweak the nips with the clamps still attached. The boy cried out in pain as the clamps continued to bite into his slaveflesh. The Leatherman's cock explored the slave's hole. Further and further it inched into the boy's interior. The boy's screams of pain could be heard even through the Leather hood.

The Leatherman began thrusting his cock vigorously into the boy. Pumping his cock into the boy's mineshaft.

The Leatherman gripped the boy's Leather-covered cheeks, pressing his own Leather-covered body against the naked flesh of the slave. Pumping. Thrusting. Arching his back. He could feel the jism rise in his own cock, edging its way to the piss slit of his cock. Pumping, thrusting, taking what was rightfully his, as the slaveowner, the boy's Master, and as a Leather fucking sadist TOP!

And he shot, a loadful up the boy's ass.

The Leatherman was sweating from the exertion. He heaved several times before withdrawing his cock from the boy's receptive hole. His cock was dripping, full of mancum. He shook his cock, dripping the residue onto the slave's back.

He heaved several more times. He went over to an outcropping of rock, settled himself against it, and watched his slave. Twisting, pulling on the ropes, moaning. The Leatherman absently played with his cock until it was restored to normal size. He soon dozed off.

From sheer exhaustion, the slave lay silently. He waited for the next assault, not aware that his Sir had fallen asleep. His body ached from the lashings. His asshole was sore from the invasion and his tits burned and ached. As the silence continued, the boy could make out faint sounds, "Birds," he thought, "Unless they know how to untie ropes, they aren't any fucking help." He struggled against the ropes, "What if Sir has left me here? Shit, I could die here... I have no idea where I am, except I'm tied to railroad tracks... What if a fucking train comes along?" The slave had no knowledge that a train no longer ran this set of tracks. He attempted to yell, but it was no good, the buttplug had his tongue held a prisoner. He struggled more. The ropes were just too tight. Sweat poured out of him – causing the flogging marks to burn. The slave began to cry.

By and by, the slave became aware of a distinct sound – not birdsong. His ears, muffled by the Leathered hood, strained to make out what it was. As he strained to hear, the sound became audible – the distinct whistle of a train.

"Oh, fuck! Get me out of here. Sir!" the boy cried out, muffled by the buttplug.

He pulled at the ropes. They cut into his flesh. At this point, he didn't care. "Rope burns will heal," the slave rationalized, "getting run over by a train..." "FUCK! SIR! Get me out of here..." the slave cried as best he could.

The train whistle sounded again. The slaveboy was sweating profusely. "Where has Sir gone?" the boyslave wondered. He began making promises to his Sir, to God, to anyone who would untie him. The ropes had now cut deep tracks in his wrists. The whistle sounded a long and mournful sound as it approached closer and closer. The boyslave continued crying, begging, praying, cursing.

Yet the train whistle was coming closer and closer. He could feel the vibrations on the tracks underneath his trussed limbs.

A steady clacking of the train's wheels could be heard in the distance. The boy struggled more and more.

The train sounded another louder whistle. It was rumbling down the tracks at break-neck speed.

The boy lost consciousness as he heard the pounding of the train's wheels on the tracks coming closer and closer.

A screeching of brakes. Metal sliding, grating against metal. The whistle blew one more time.

"Holy fucking hell, what the hell…?" the engineer questioned as he pulled the emergency brake system. He rubbed his eyes.

He, and the others on the train, climbed down from the train.

A naked boy was tied to the tracks.

The boy woke sometime later. He felt paralyzed. "Am I alive?" He was lying facedown. He tried to move his arms and legs but could not. He reared his head up, but all he could see was a pair of boots.

"Well, well, well, the boy is coming to…" a man's voice said.

Before he could rationalize his situation, a violent thrust of manhood assaulted his boyhole.

He reared his head up again, screaming.

"Relax, boy," a voice, apparently attached to the boots, said.

The boy mumbled something, but the buttplug was still in his mouth.

A rough hand reached down and pulled the plug out of his mouth.

"Where am I?" the boy weakly asked.

"You're on the ghost train, boy," another voice responded. A peal of laughter broke forth from at least five or six different directions. "We ride these tracks searching for slaveboys just like you. Left behind by their sadistic Masters." Another healthy round of laughter erupted. The boy caught glimpses of the men through the eye slits in his Leather hood. They were all dressed in head-to-toe Leather, but covered in layers of grime. Old Leather – turned rusty brown from years of hard service. The men's faces were covered in soot. Big handlebar mustaches and muttonchop sideburns. Most were smoking a half-burned stogie.

The thrusting of the mancock continued, in and out of his hole. Finally, with a mighty thrust, warm cum rushed into the boy's innards.

"Let me up from here," the boy pleaded.

"We ain't through with you, yet," a voice said as the boy felt the man's cock withdrew from his fuckhole.

Another one took its place. And another. The boy was assaulted so many times he lost count. He lapsed into unconsciousness.

The men hooted. They slapped the boy's ass repeatedly. After they shot their loads, they massaged their cocks into fullness before aiming their swollen cocks toward the boy. A communal pissing. As he woke from unconsciousness, the boy was still laying face down as the toe of a boot lifted his chin. "Lick my boot, boy." The boot was filthy, covered in soot and dirt. The boy complied with the remaining strength he had.

As each boot was serviced, another boot took its place, presenting itself for servicing by the boy's tongue.

The train's men didn't notice that a new passenger had boarded the train.

"He's my boyslave and you can't have him yet," said the Leatherman. A heavy flogger was positioned in his right hand.

The train men shrank from the Leatherman's presence.

"Ah, hell, we was just havin' a little fun with your boy," the engineer attempted to explain.

"SHUT THE FUCK UP! He's my slave and you can't have him yet." With that the Leatherman reached down and untied the boy's feet. He lifted the boy to a standing position, but the boy started to sink down to his knees. The Leatherman pulled him up once again.

Holding the boy's bound hands, the Leatherman escorted the boy off the train. As soon as the feet of the Leatherman and his slave touched the ground, the train and its crew vanished into thin air.

The boy was kneeling, although he was swaying. The Leatherman flogged him several times. "You're not allowed to service any other man unless I order you to…" and with that, the Leatherman flogged him until his back and ass were bloodied.

"Now get down and lick your Master's boots, slave."

Snatched from the transporters of death and glad to be alive, the slave gratefully licked his Master's boots.

THE EMERGENCE OF
A LEATHERMAN

Dedicated to Pete, my sexy redhaired Leatherbuddy.

Pete did not consider himself attractive. When he looked in the mirror each morning, he saw a hairline beginning to recede, green eyes (he thought blue eyes were far sexier), a snub nose, a gap between his front teeth, and worst of all, that damned red beard and mustache. He hated red hair! He had almost shaved off both beard and mustache several times. He had once dyed his mustache (when he didn't have a beard) black – it looked ridiculous! He looked like the dictator of a foreign country. God, how he envied guys with black, sexy hair. Lots of black hair on their chest and around their cocks. Instead, he had a red bush of hair.

While looking in the mirror, though, Pete did admire his trim body. He ran every morning and weightlifted. He did have really nice pecs if he did say so himself.

Pete had a rare Saturday off. He worked a lot of weekends and as a result, he didn't have a large circle of friends. He was a loner, by nature. He put on his tight white tee shirt and similarly-tight blue jeans. As he laced his jogging shoes into place, he thought about his sister's impending wedding. He needed a gift and he needed a suit – it was to be a toney affair with a reception at the Country Club. Jeans and tee shirts would be frowned upon. He began to stroll through the downtown. He really did want to get his sister something nice, but affordable. As Pete slowly walked past the shops, he attempted to catch the eye of several cute guys but they seemed to look right through him. As if he was transparent. The street was lined with specialty shops and Pete ducked into quite a few. He rejected a crystal vase (too conventional), a small painting of a snow-covered field (impressionistic, beautiful, but expensive!) and a patchwork quilt (even more expensive!).

He came upon a shop with the name *Second Hand Rose's Second Chance Tschotske Shop.* "What the hell?" Pete thought as he entered. He was warmly greeted by a woman, bohemian in dress, but very friendly. Pete thought, "She's just one of those people you instantly like – you want to buy something from her, because she is so nice."

The stock was definitely bohemian as well, reflecting many decades past and the poor taste exhibited during those decades. "God," thought Pete, "I wouldn't give this crap to my worst enemy." To be polite, however, he continued to look through the extensive shop. He felt compelled to buy something.

As he continued to the back of the store, the inventory switched to vintage clothing. The discarded prom dresses and ruffled tuxedo shirts of days gone by. The shop had a small men's section and Pete headed there. He found the inevitable polyester suits, wide, boldly-colored ties, and pairs of white shoes. As he absently thumbed through the suits, he had little hope of finding a suit that he could wear to the wedding. But still he continued. As he slid hanger after hanger on the rack, he pulled into view a well-worn motorcycle jacket. His hand caressed the soft Leather – it was like butter. The black Leather had acquired a patina which blended from soft greyish black to reddish-brown highlights. Pete took it off the hanger and tried it on. He zipped up the zipper and belted the belt. It… was a perfect fit. He wore it to the front of the store, seeking a mirror.

The transformation was remarkable. The jacket fit perfectly – sleeve length, chest size. The reddish-brown highlights of the jacket somehow made his beard and mustache look sexy. Attractive. "Fucking hot," he concluded. He preened in the mirror – viewing himself from the left, looking over his shoulder, flipping up the collar, sticking his hands in the zippered pockets.

He quickly realized that his cock supported the acquisition of the Leather jacket. It was pressing against the crotch of his jeans. Just as he realized this, a voice behind him said, "Darling, it was as if that jacket was made for you. You look devilishly handsome..." Pete was fairly certain that the shopkeeper was being sincere and not just trying to make another sale.

"You really think so?" Pete said, not taking his eyes off himself.

"Darling," she clucked, "if I was forty years younger..." She squeezed his asscheek and laughed.

Needless to say, a sale was made. The lady even deducted $20 from the price. Impulsively, Pete leaned over and kissed Rose on the cheek.

"Let me fold it up," she said as she opened a shopping bag.

"Oh... no... I'd like to wear it home."

"As you wish, dear. Come back and see me." Pete assured her he would.

Pete emerged on the street. The jacket hugged his body. Its tightness rubbed against his easily-aroused nipples. He could feel his aroused cock straining against the denim of the blue jeans. As he walked down the street, he noticed a few men smiling... at him! One good-looking man, momentarily standing in a doorway, quietly said, "Leatherman. Yum – hot." Pete smiled as he continued walking. Pete felt hotter and hotter as he sauntered down the street. Men were looking at him.

He arrived back in his apartment and stripped off his clothes. He put the jacket back on and looked at himself in the mirror. Fuck, he was handsome. The jacket showed off his masculine chest so, so nicely. He pulled out a pair of black Leather dress gloves and put them on.

"Holy Shit, this looks great." The tight black Leathered fingers pulled on his cock's shaft.

He climbed on the bed and continued pulling on his cock, which was already arching upward.

The Leather jacket enveloped him. His gloves pulled on the shaft of his cock. He began to fantasize that it was a handsome, young man doing the yanking of his rod.

"Go down on my cock, boy," he instructed the imaginary boy.

The willing boy began tonguing Pete's cock.

"Do it more vigorously, boy," he again instructed the imaginary submissive. He yanked on his cock with his right hand, pulling his balls with his left hand.

His cock swelled under the intense stroking and he soon shot a load. He licked the cum off his gloves.

Pete wore the jacket and gloves to bed that night.

The next morning was a Sunday and so, Pete stayed in bed a good long time, pulling the jacket tightly around him, rubbing his nipples with the jacket.

"Fuck, this is what I've been missing for so long," Pete thought to himself.

He climbed out of bed and stood in front of the mirror. The Leather jacket looked damned good. He stroked his beard. "You are one sexy fucker," he said to himself, who nodded an approval in the mirror.

His cock also voted its approval by arching upward.

Pete decided to go for a walk in his newly-found Leather. Putting the same outfit on from yesterday, he strutted down the street. Once more, men looked at him with smiles and nods of the head.

As he continued, a group of bikers rolled down the street. Leather from head to toe.

"Fuck!" Pete remarked as he instinctively grabbed his crotch. Realizing where he was, he quickly withdrew his hand, but the hard cock pushed against the denim.

One detail that he noticed was that none of the men wore jogging shoes. They all wore heavy boots.

"Damn," he thought, "that's what I need."

He knew there was a shoe store some blocks away. "I could go back and get my car, or I could walk."

He walked, he wanted to be admired. He just hoped that no one would look at his feet.

The shoe store did not have men's boots, but the store clerk advised him of a bootery a few more blocks away. The clerk knew for a fact that the bootery was open until five on a Sunday. He walked, continuing to elicit nods of approval from men who were out enjoying the scenery, including the handsome young man strutting past them in a Leather jacket. The approval was powerful. He only wished that he was walking down the street with that imaginary submissive trailing behind him. Maybe on a leash!

After getting lost several times, Pete found the bootery. The smell of black Leather was overpowering. Cowboy boots, engineer boots, construction boots. Pete wanted to stick his face in each one, absorbing the aroma.

As if drawn to a particular section of the store, he found a section of logger boots. Wescos. Lace-ups. Knee-high. He didn't have to look any further.

A half-hour later, Pete emerged with a bag. The bag contained his old jogging shoes. He proudly wore his new loggers. Laced up to the knee – his asstight blue jeans tucked neatly into the tops of the boots. Fuck, he felt powerful.

Even more men were now looking at him as he marched down the street. Arriving back at his apartment, he looked at himself in the mirror. He stared at himself for a long time. He was fucking hot and he knew it. He once again crawled onto the bed and began a delicious jack-off session. He fantasized that a boy was tonguing his boots, making sure to clean every inch.

As soon as he thought about a cute boy with his head bobbing in between his legs, Pete could not control his seed, and soon, shot a load of cum with the help of his gloved hands.

The next few days passed quickly at work because he knew that his Leather would be waiting for him when he got home. He couldn't wait to put it on.

Saturday night arrived and Pete was already suited up. The Wescos felt as if he had them for years instead of just a week. The jacket, of course, felt the same way. Pete had just climbed onto his bed when his cellphone rang.

Answering the phone, it was his old friend Jim.

"Hey, Buddy, what are you doing tonight?"

"Just spending some time by myself," Pete answered. He really didn't want to be bothered in his silent reverie of Leather and cock worship.

"A group of us are headed to 'The Den' – you want to go?"

'The Den' was a gay bar.

"Oh, Jim, I don't know…" Pete began.

"Oh, come on, you spend too much time alone. They've got dancers."

"Oh, I don't know, Jim, I'm not in the mood to look at dancers tonight." He just wanted to play with himself.

"It's also Leather-Levi night."

"What? When did they start that?"

"You are behind the times… about a month ago."

"Hmmm… I might come. I'll join you there."

"Okay, Buddy," Jim said, and hung up.

Pete began manipulating his cock. It was already aroused by the Leather which hugged and caressed his body. The thought of seeing other guys in Leather made him even hornier. He tugged on his cock, pulling his balls with the other hand. Reaching up, twisting his erect nipples. He thought of the fucking hot bikers he had seen. Leather stretched tightly across their muscular backs. Leather stretched at the knee, disappearing into a pair of black Leather boots. Leather crotch stretched across the cycle's seat. Black Leather covering their handsome asses. He began moaning as his cock felt the urge to jack. He stroked it from head to the bottom of the shaft. Squeezing his balls, twisting his nips. Feeling the soft Leather against his skin. "Fuck, yeah, this Leatherman is going to the bar."

Pete decided to wear the jacket, jeans, and boots. Gloves too. No shirt. He wanted the guys to see his handsome chest, despite the red hair on it.

Pete left his apartment around 10. The bar was about twenty miles away and so, he drove. He found a parking space near the bar and as he climbed out of the car, there were three Leatherguys talking outside of the bar.

As he walked to the bar, the guys watched his approach.

He felt good, he felt confident. For the first time in a long time, he felt sexy.

He nodded to the guys.

"Good Evening, Sir," two of them responded. The third said, "How's it hanging, Buddy?" All three wore cycle jackets, harnesses, Leather pants, and biker boots. Only the third man wore a Muir cap, pulled low over his forehead.

Thinking quickly, he responded, "It's ready to plow an ass."

The guys laughed and he went into the bar. The bar was dark. The crowd was light, with a number of guys in bar vests and tee shirts. He ordered a beer and retreated to a corner. Jim and the others had not made an appearance. Pete made a mental note to find a Muir cap to add to his newly-acquired wardrobe. The Leatherman looked very authoritative in it – pulled low over his forehead.

As he ordered a second beer, he noticed that the three guys were now in the bar, a cluster of men around them. He didn't feel quite confident enough to break into the conversation and so, he returned to the corner. He casually looked over several times where the three Leatherguys were still surrounded.

By and by, however, the guys scattered leaving the three men. The Leatherman with the Muir cap sauntered over to the bar, followed by the two other guys. They placed their drink orders.

After receiving their drinks, the man in the Muir cap led the way. They headed straight for Pete's corner.

"No need to worry, Buddy," the man in the Muir cap stated, "the crowd will thicken. You'll have your pick. I'm Master David."

"Good to meet you, I'm Pete," as they shook hands.

"These are my boys Rob and Hank."

Pete extended his hand, but the boys' hands remained behind their backs. He quickly withdrew his hand, hoping that they had not noticed.

"You been here before, Pete?"

"It's been awhile…"

"You traveling solo tonight? Your boy didn't come with you…"

"No," Pete replied. Thinking fast, he added, "He's being punished at home... in my dungeon."

"Yep," Master David, "you have to discipline them every once in awhile just to show them who is boss, huh?" He took a swig of beer. Apparently they took Pete for a top and he was relishing that role. Now, if it was only true.

The conversation continued. Master David said, "I'm gonna retreat to the back patio so I can light up. Want to join me?"

"Be glad to, Buddy," Pete replied as the four headed to the patio.

Hank held the door for his Master and Pete. There were more guys out on the patio all smoking like fiends. A 'no smoking' policy inside the bar had forced the men outside.

Master David extracted a large cigar from his inner pocket. Pete slapped his pocket and remarked, "Damn! Must have left my cigar case at home."

"Not a problem, Buddy, try one of mine," Master David replied as he extracted another cigar from his inner pocket.

Pete began unwrapping the cigar from its cellophane enclosure, but Master David interrupted the procedure, "Let my boy do it for you."

Pete handed the cigar to Rob. He carefully unwrapped the cigar, pulled a cigar clip from his bar vest, clipped it, and pulled out a box of wooden matches.

He presented the cigar to Pete. Pete, following the lead of Master David, placed it squarely in his mouth and waited for the boy to light the match.

Fortunately, Pete drew on the strong cigar lightly and didn't choke.

Master David clicked his fingers and Hank dropped on all fours. Master David propped his booted foot on the back of the boy. Rob watched Pete carefully. Following suit, Pete motioned for Rob to fall on all fours and soon his Wescoed foot rested on the boy's back.

Master David stoked the cigar in his mouth for some time. Pete followed his lead. He was getting the hang of this.

"So…," Master David began, "what do you like to do to a boy?"

Thinking quickly and having viewed a few porn flicks in his day, he responded, "Work 'em over. Tie 'em up and fuck their ass with a greased-up dildo, followed by my own cock."

"Yeah, it keeps those boys in line, doesn't it?" Master David replied, "When they're all trussed up and at your mercy. You hood your boys?"

"Fuck, yeah. That way they don't know what to expect." Pete added a Leather hood to his list of equipment needed. Along with a cigar case, and a supply of cigars.

The men continued to converse while the boys calmly remained in the sub position. Men were filtering in and out, some watching the four. Pete was enjoying every second.

Pete's mind was fast-forwarding at this point and thought of an idea to impress Master David.

He removed his foot from Rob's back and commanded "Up, boy!"

The boy rose and placed his hands behind his back.

"Taste my ash, boy." as he pulled the boy's jaw down and flicked the extended ash on the boy's tongue. The boy chewed it slowly and swallowed.

"Thank you, Sir." Pete had read that in an article about ashtray service.

Seeming to follow Pete's head, Master David did the same.

"Pete, why don't you come back to my dungeon? I've been looking for another top to assist me. Let's work over these boys."

Pete didn't give it a second thought. The thought of working over one of these boys was too good to be true.

"Sure. Sounds like a fucking good idea."

As the four headed back through the bar, the boys following behind Master David and Pete, Pete spotted Jim.

"I'll be just a minute, Buddy, have to say hello to an old friend."

Pete walked over to Jim who looked astonished.

"For someone who said you might not come, you made up for it. Look at you, when did you get those Leathers?"

"I can't talk now, Jim. Got some action. And Jim… get your ass in Leather." Jim was wearing shorts and a Hawaiian shirt.

Jim was further astounded. He couldn't think of a reply as Pete headed out of the bar with the three men in Leather.

Pete followed in his car. The lead car led through a series of streets and left and right turns. He was beginning to doubt his pursuit of this conquest. What if Master David tied him up? Pete had no experience in S&M beyond what he viewed in porn flicks. A couple of times the seeds of doubt swirled around in his head. But, then he thought about those two cute Leather boys, willing to kneel at his feet, willing to take his ash. He wanted this experience so he kept following Master David's car closely. Finally, they arrived at a respectable looking townhouse in the middle of the city. He exited the car, smoking on his cigar, pulling on his tightening crotch.

Master David sent the boys downstairs, presumably to the dungeon. He offered Pete another beer, which Pete willingly took to calm his nerves.

"The boys will be ready in a few minutes – they know my routine."

Master David led Pete down to the dungeon. Pete's eyes widened and he started sweating. He had never seen so many devices in one place. He didn't know what some of them were for.

"This is a great set-up," Pete professed, "it makes my dungeon look primitive." He thought to himself, "I don't even have a dungeon. And just where will I put that in my apartment?"

The boys were now naked, except for their boots. They knelt with their heads bowed and their arms behind their backs.

"Which one do you want to work over first?" Master David offered.

They were both attractive, muscular, firm nips, cute asses.

Pete wavered in his decision, finally pointing to Hank.

"Go at him, Buddy."

Pete swaggered over to Hank, standing behind him. He pulled the boy's face backward by his jaw.

"All right, boy, I'm gonna work you over because you're a worthless piece of shit."

"Yes, Sir. Thank you, Sir," Hank replied.

He slapped the boy's cheek with his gloved hand. Damn, he thought, that felt good. He slapped the boy several more times. Each time the boy thanked him.

Master David handed him bondage rope and Pete proceeded to loop the rope around the boy's chest, over his arms, under his arms, eventually layering the ropes tightly around the boy's upper arms. He maneuvered the boy's arms so that they were bent at the elbows, hugging his ribcage. Pete tied it off around the boy's waist and then around his crotch.

"Interesting," Master David commented, "you've done this a few times before."

Pete was reveling in the praise, but simply nodded. He thought that his nervous voice would give him away.

He then selected a Leather hood from a shelf of toys. He laced the hood tightly in place.

"Against the wall, boy," Pete demanded.

"Yes, Sir," Hank replied. Pete guided him to the wall and made him face it. The wall had two waist-high rings embedded into it and so, Pete placed a pair of cuffs on the boy's wrists and then connected them to the rings with S hooks.

He then selected a paddle off the shelf.

He tested it the first few times with light taps.

"My boys are used to much more…" Master David commented.

"Don't worry," Pete said, as he began to beat the boy's ass with more power. After all, he was a weightlifter. He knew that he had struck 'a chord' when the boy began flinching. "Take it, boy." he yelled. He was really getting into it. His cock had already hardened in his pants. He struck with more force, counting the strikes. He gave the boy seventy-five whacks. The boy's ass was reddened at the end of the first rotation.

By this point, Pete's cigar was nothing but a stub.

Master David had not commandeered Rob and so, Pete ordered Rob to fetch him a cigar. Master David has been leaning against a post, observing Pete's technique and rubbing his crotch. The boy obligingly retrieved a cigar and soon, Pete was puffing away at a second cigar.

"Work this boy over now, Pete, while I attend to your first subject," Master David offered.

Master David stood behind Hank and pulling off his cod, inserted his cock into Hank's service area.

Pete selected a ball gag from the shelf and buckled it tightly around Rob's jaw.

He led Rob to the St. Andrew's cross which stood in the center of the room.

Rob was quickly manacled to the cross and the paddling from Pete began.

Rob's ass was apparently more sensitive and the boy began flinching almost immediately. He moaned as each strike hit his ass. "Fuck, this is wonderful! Two boys in one fucking night," Pete thought.

While Pete's cock was throbbing in his jeans, Master David was pumping his loaded cock into Hank's hole. Pete looked over, distracted by the beautiful sight of Master's David's Leather-covered ass flexing as he pumped with ferocity.

"Damn, I can do that too!" he thought.

He unzipped his jeans and extracted his heated-up meat. He spit on it to lubricate the shaft. He spread the boy's reddened asscheeks and guided his cock up the boy's hole.

"This feels so fucking good," Pete thought as his cock made its way up the fuckhole. The boy arched his ass upward to accommodate the manrod.

Pete began a slow pumping, hoping to prolong the sensation. He was just too excited and he quickly came. He stood with his cock still inserted in the boy's hole, looking over to view his fellow Leatherman. Master David was still drilling Hank's hole. He was pulling on Hank's dick with one hand and pulling on the boy's nipples with the other. Alternating hands.

His Leathered body slammed against the boy's naked flesh. "Fuck!" yelled Master David as he apparently climaxed. The boy's body slammed against the wall, his chest heaving.

Pete pulled out and wiped the cum with his gloved hand. He presented it to the boy after he had removed the ball gag. The boy licked it eagerly, thanking him several times.

Master David finally pulled his cock out, but licked the cum himself.

"I don't let my boys taste my cum until the third fucking for the night," Master David explained.

Pete's dick was spent for the moment and he began sweating again. "Three sessions," he thought, "can I do it? Shit! I'll prove myself as a Leatherman if I do. Wish I had just a little time for my cock to reconnect with my newly-found S&M pleasures."

"Let's go upstairs for a beer and let the boys rest."

Pete breathed an inner sigh of relief.

The sessions continued with Pete performing well. The boys' backs and asses were crisscrossed with red flogging marks. Their asses and mouths oozed jism from two Leathermen's cocks. The boys gratefully took cigar ash and served as footstools for the remainder of the evening. Pete finally left at 4 AM. And so it was, that Pete emerged as a red-hot, red-haired Leatherdaddy.

SNOWBOUND

When the Leatherboy arrived, his Leatherdaddy was shoveling snow. The Leatherdaddy wore a pair of Carhartt coveralls. The only indication that he was a Leatherman was his motorcycle hat, black Leather gloves, his shitkicker Engineer's boots, and a big cigar clenched between his teeth.

The man and boy worked side by side until a path had been shoveled to the toolshed.

"In, boy," as the Leatherman unlocked the door.

The boy knew the routine and laid down on the table, facing the ceiling.

Leatherdaddy stood in front of his boy. The boy's cock hardened as the Leatherman unzipped his Carhartts, revealing a Leather harness, a loaded Leather jock, and his Leather chaps. The top of the Leatherman's mushroom-headed cock throbbed above the top of the jockstrap and the boy knew he was in for a rewarding session.

The Daddy retrieved a cat o'nine tails flogger from the D ring of the waistband of his chaps.

"Are you ready, boy?" as the Leatherdaddy clamped his Leather gloved hand over the boy's mouth and nostrils.

As the boy lost consciousness, he felt his Daddy climb onto the table.

He woke sometime later to the sensation that he was being violated. Daddy's big cock was inserted in the boy's asshole and the boy's legs were draped over the man's muscular shoulders. The boy's chest was being flogged repeatedly by the cat o'nine tails. The metal tips left a delicious sting each time they struck.

Daddy's cock was huge and was painful as it inched up the boy's rectum. The Daddy leaned down and blew smoke in the boy's face.

"Have a nice nap, Leatherboy?" the Daddy snarled, as he thrust his cock into the boy's hole.

"Yes, Daddy," the boy winced as he responded.

"This is only the beginning, boy."

The boy thought his insides would burst as the Daddy continued to assault him.

After a length of time, the man abruptly pulled out his juiced-up cock.

He rubbed it on his Leather fist and then proceeded to insert two, then four fingers and finally his whole Leathered fist up the raw territory. Despite the boy's pain, his own cock was hardening.

The Leatherdaddy surveyed the hardened cock and laid the flogger aside.

His other Leathered glove hand pulled savagely on the boy's cock, until the boy thought his cock would be pulled off.

As if reading the boy's thoughts, the Leatherdaddy just laughed.

"This is not frat boy sex, boy, this is S&M man sex, and you are my fuck pig."

The Leatherman continued.

"Oh, Daddy, I'm goin' to shoot..." as the boy grimaced.

"Don't you shoot, boy, until I tell you to..." Despite the warning, the boy shot a load of cum on the man's Leathered glove and on his Leather-covered thigh.

"You fucked up, boy!" the Leatherdaddy yelled, and slapped the boy across the face with his gloved hand. He wiped the boy's cum on the boy's face and then made the boy lick the glove and then around his mouth.

The Leatherdaddy picked up his flogger and flogged the boy's cock. The boy's cock shrunk, but the Daddy manipulated it until it was semi-hard.

"You won't fuck up again." With that, the Daddy flipped the boy over on the table.

The boy's ankles were placed in ankle restraints. The Daddy lifted the boy's booted feet off the end of the table and hooked the boot restraints to the chains suspended from the ceiling. The boy's wrists were quickly placed in wrist restraints and chained to the sides of the table.

The Leatherdaddy pulled a large Leather paddle off the side table and beat the boy's ass until it was raw. He then flogged the boy's ass until it had a crisscrossing of red marks across it. The Daddy stood beside the table as he then administered the flogger to the boy's back.

The boy groaned as each lashing intensified. The boy could feel his cock hardening once again.

As if reading the boy's thoughts, the man said, "You're gettin' hard again, aren't you, boy?

"Yes, Sir, please let me up, Sir, and I will service your cock..." The boy lifted his head and turned it pleadingly to the Daddy.

"You'll do that when I tell you to do that, fuck boy."

He pushed the boy's head down on the table. The Leatherdaddy covered the boy's head in a black Leather hood with openings for his nostrils. He pinched the nostrils tightly and the boy lost consciousness once again.

The Daddy exited the toolshed but returned a short time later with a roll of plastic wrap.

Pretty soon, the boy was trussed in shoulder to toe wrapping, bound tightly. His arms, released from the restraints, were tightly bound to his sides. The Daddy had further wrapped the boy's neck and lower jaw.

When the boy woke, he couldn't move. He was immobilized and was once again lying on his stomach.

The boy panicked because, out of the corner of his eye, he could see that the Leatherdaddy was brandishing a short-handled knife.

The Daddy crawled on top of the boy and carefully slit an opening in the plastic wrap at the boy's asshole. He quickly inserted his big handsome dick into the plastic wrapping and into the boy's fuckhole.

With that, the Leatherdaddy engaged in a frenzied pumping of his cock, until he shot his cock's load into the boy's hole. He resealed the slit. The boy was moaning from all the activity.

The boy's hardening cock throbbed against the plastic wrapping. The man lifted his boy once again and threw him ass downward on the table.

The Leatherdaddy picked up the knife. The boy panicked momentarily but knew that his Daddy wouldn't slice off any essential parts.

Precum had collected at the head of the boy's cock With that, the Leatherdaddy slit a long gash and the boy's cock sprang upward. It shot a cumload skyward.

Even the Daddy was impressed and he sat on top of his boy, smearing the boy's cum on the boy's face.

"Good boy," the Leatherman remarked.

"Next time it snows, boy, we'll do this again," the Leatherdaddy promised. He began unwrapping his boy.

The boy began stretching his neck from side to side. As he did so, he glimpsed the first flakes of snow settling on the windowsill.

The boy lost consciousness without any help from the Leatherdaddy.

The Leatherdaddy sighed and exited to his kitchen for another roll of plastic wrap.

SUBMIT

A new life. Starting over. Seemingly from scratch. Take advice from me – your life can change in an instant.

My Master Dan and I had been together for fourteen years until the unthinkable happened. Dan was killed in a motorcycle accident. I witnessed the head-on collision. We were out for a ride on a crisp fall afternoon. A truck rounded the curve on our side of the road. Dan was the lead cycle and had no time to react. As I slowly recuperated in a therapy room for weeks, my mind reran the horrible accident over. And over. And over.

When I was able to return to the house that we shared, Dan's presence was everywhere. His well-polished boots. His favorite flogger. Even his cigar butt in the ashtray. I packed his Leather items up and stored them. That did little good. His presence was still so strong. I dismantled the dungeon in which we had played. I no longer had an interest in anything that reminded me of the pleasure he received from the pain he administered. He was a good Master and I was his devoted submissive.

I put the house on the market and moved to the west coast. A new life. Starting over...

Trevor Edwin Strickland was twenty-five. A young buck. Proud of his accomplishments. Graduated near the top of his class from Graduate School and was already offered three jobs, the least of which would afford him a nice house, frequent trips to exotic places, sporty cars (and a motorcycle!), and any boyfriend he wanted. Trevor was also proud of his gayness and his willingness to experiment with 'alternate' forms of his own sexuality. He was drawn to the intriguing world of sadomasochism. He had very little experience with it beyond being tied up in a friend's garage. But he had already visited the Leather bars in D.C. and the cock in his pants told him that it was more than a passing interest in jamming his ass in Leather and submitting to one of the powerful, intimidating Daddy-types who lurked in the dark corners of the bar, looking for suitable prey.

Trevor began looking for a house in the trendy suburbs of Washington. The exorbitant price range did nothing to dissuade him from looking in Georgetown, Alexandria, et al. The realtor was exasperated after having shown him approximately thirty different properties all of which had been rejected for various reasons by the arrogant young man. Still, his bank references had clearly shown that he was pulling down a six figure salary and could 'put his money where his mouth was."

"If you head a little further north, I think you will find something suitable..." the realtor Phyllis suggested.

"I'm not opposed to that as long as it's not too far away from metro D.C..."

An email in early August from Mr. Stone, simply saying, "Any bites?" reminded Phyllis of a property that might fill the bill. Phyllis had forgotten about the former Martin-Stone house. It had been on the market for close to two years. Not one solid offer. Yet, it was a really decent house, lots of room, lots of privacy. Maybe the self-assured Mr. Strickland would like to see it. The house was a little over the top – Second Empire, mansard roof. Cast-iron fencing surrounding the property. Slightly foreboding – but that was, Phyllis supposed, because it had not been lived in for two years. The owner had been killed in a motorcycle accident and his partner had moved away. A little landscaping and some sprucing up and it would come alive again.

She placed a call to Strickland and he agreed to see it. Phyllis continued to hype the amenities of the property as she firmed up their agreement to meet the following Tuesday.

As they toured the house, Trevor was impressed by all he saw. A white and black marble tile flooring in the front hallway. A fireplace in the living suite, with walk-in closets on either side. "One could be a humidor," Trevor mused. As was his new station in life, he had recently taken up smoking illicit Cuban cigars. "The rooms have wall-space for canvases," Trevor remarked, as he envisioned bold paintings featuring male nudes, bulging muscles, huge cocks. He added that to his list of 'needs'. Now that he was making big money, he wanted to become known as a connoisseur of fine art.

They continued the tour. A modern kitchen with all the amenities. As Phyllis led the young man downstairs to the basement, Trevor envisioned a well-stocked wine cellar. As they explored the second floor, Trevor was impressed with the Master Bedroom which also was equipped with a fireplace. French doors led to a private balcony looking out over the backyard. Four more bedrooms, "one of which could be turned into a library – lined with Leather-bound volumes... smoking a cigar while reading the classics." Trevor was drawn to the house like no other.

"I want it," he succinctly stated to the realtor, as she muttered "Thank God!" under her breath.

Less than two months later, Trevor Strickland entered his new home with the keys to his new house jingling in his hand.

He had ordered furnishings for the house. They had been placed within the house under the supervision of an interior decorator hired by Trevor. He wanted his first night in the house to appear as if he had always lived there. He excitedly ran from room to room to see the work of Stephen, the decorator. Trevor made a short list of minor changes or minor details to be addressed.

The bedroom was particularly handsome. Mr. Strickland had even commissioned a portrait of himself. It was now placed over the fireplace in the bedroom.

"You handsome devil," Trevor remarked as he looked up into the eyes of his portrait.

"Congratulations, Lord of the Manor." the portrait seemed to respond.

A bottle of champagne was chilling in the refrigerator. Trevor uncorked it with a satisfying 'pop' and toasted his new home. He carried the champagne and glass up to his new library, still devoid of the books he would acquire on future trips to antique stores and auctions. He selected a cigar from a table-top humidor and settled in for the night.

Trevor woke with a start. He was slumped down in his library chair. The cigar was half-smoked, resting in the crystal ashtray. The champagne bottle was nearly empty.

Momentarily, Trevor did not recognize the surroundings.

"Ah, yes. My Library…" He readied himself for bed and crawled into his four-postered bed for a night of restful sleep.

Trevor once again woke with a start. Had someone said something? He attempted to pull his slumbering mind into wakefulness. He thought he had heard a man's voice. "Must have been a dream," he rationalized as he fell quickly back to sleep.

The next several nights passed quickly, but each night, he woke with a start. Each night his brain registered a man's voice. Close enough to sound as if was next to him, but never close enough to determine what the man's voice was saying.

Trevor held an open house one month from the day he had been handed the keys. The house was filled with affluent young men, all gay of course. He had acquired the services of several young men who were serving as bartenders and servers. They wore bowties and black Leather jockstraps. Trevor himself was dressed in a black Leather tuxedo – another luxury afforded by his high-paying salary. Champagne and liquor flowed. Cigar smoke was heavy throughout the house. Hors d'oeuvres were served by the cute young men, who were subjected to having their buttcheeks pinched and their jockstraps tweaked. Yes, it was a party to remember. Trevor finally crawled into bed at 4:30 AM. Unfortunately, he had not retained the services of one of the cute young men so he slept alone. He quickly fell into a deep sleep.

He woke suddenly as he felt the sharp slap of a hand across his cheek.

"Whaat?" he yelled, as he sat up in bed. Yet, to all appearances, he was alone. He groggily stumbled to the bathroom and looked at his bleary-eyed self in the mirror. The distinct reddened outline of a hand appeared on his left cheek.

"What the hell?" as he ran into the bedroom. He looked in the closets and ran down the stairs. No one appeared to be in the house except himself. Placing his hand on his cheek, he still felt the sting of the handprint on his cheek.

"I must be dreaming," as he crawled into bed.

Trevor slept until the early afternoon. As he entered the bathroom, he looked in the mirror. There was no handprint. Trevor dismissed it as a bad dream – too much booze or too much cigar smoke.

The next several days at work were brutal and Trevor often did not return before nine at night. A quick shower and he was usually too tired to do anything except drink a glass of wine, smoke half a cigar and crawl into bed. The day's work crowded into his subconscious as he reviewed the pile of work he had to complete. He often woke in the middle of the night, feeling as if a heavy weight was pressing down on his body. He attributed this to the stress he was feeling until the project was completed and it could be shipped off to its next stage of development. On Thursday night, he returned. The project was mostly completed and he relaxed in his library for a good hour before retiring. He knew he would sleep well this night. He fell into a deep sleep. Halfway through the night, he woke. He attempted to move, but it felt as if his hands were being held down. A full force held his body immobilized. As he strove toward full consciousness, he distinctly felt someone – ON TOP OF HIM! He struggled, but whoever it was held him firmly down. It was then that a voice whispered in his ear, "Submit…"

"What the hell?" he yelled.

"Scream all you want, boy, it's just you and me." Trevor's eyes strained to see who his assailant was, but the room was in darkness. The shadowy outline of a man was on top of him. He could just make out a man's face with black beard, mustache, and a Muir cap pulled low over the man's eyes.

"Who…are you? What do you want? How did…?" he started, but a gloved hand clamped over his mouth. With his free hand, Trevor flailed at the assailant, but it connected with no one else. His hand simply slammed into his own chest.

"How could that be possible?" Trevor attempted to rationalize.

"You'll learn, boy…" the voice continued to taunt. A mouth soon covered Trevor's mouth and a tongue reached far into Trevor's mouth. Teeth clamped onto his lips and tongue. The mouth tasted strongly of cigar smoke. A fleshy cock was soon rubbing itself against Trevor's cock and despite his fear, Trevor's cock responded.

Trevor's hands were held in place as the assailant continued to rub his hardening cock against Trevor's. The mouth continued to cover Trevor's mouth. Trevor continued to struggle against the assailant whose body was now rubbing against Trevor's naked chest. He could tell that the man was wearing a Leather jacket. Leathered legs were pinning his own legs against them.

"Submit to me, boy," as the Leathered assailant had his way with Trevor.

The Leather intruder continued a frenzied pumping until Trevor could feel the release of his own man juices and the assailant's cum pour forth onto his belly.

"Aaahh!" the Leather intruder sighed. He seemingly disappeared and Trevor fell back to sleep.

When he woke the next morning, Trevor was slow to rise. His body had gotten quite a work out. Dried cum appeared on his belly. As he crawled into the shower, he noticed the imprint of hands around his wrists. His mouth was sore, with several bite marks attesting to its soreness.

"How did someone get in? Must have had a key. Time to change the locks." Over the weekend, Trevor called in a locksmith and had every lock changed.

It was to no avail. The following week, Trevor was visited by the Leatherclad visitor. Always waking him in the middle of the night. Always holding him down in bed and having his way with Trevor. The sessions varied. Sometimes Trevor felt the sting of a whip on his flesh. The sharp sting of a gloved hand across his face. Each morning,

Trevor woke and found evidence of the nightly visitor, but no doors or windows were disturbed. Could the man be getting in through a secret entrance? How could Trevor tell the police about an intruder if he had no evidence beyond the handprints that appeared on his body? Despite his fear, Trevor had to admit that he was aroused by the mysterious lover. He enjoyed the rawness of the sessions. Rough, man sex. The exhilaration of being taken by force. He enjoyed the sensation of a Leathered body on top of him – but who the hell was it? This was in his own house.

Two weeks elapsed with nightly visits. Finally, Trevor attempted to stay awake and confront the Leatherman. It was around 2:30 AM when Trevor was drowsing. He felt the weight of the man crawling on top of him.

He sat bolt upright, "Who the hell are you?"

An evil chuckle was the only response he got, before he was thrown on his back. He could feel a rope restraint tying his left wrist to the bedpost. He attempted to strike the man in the head, but his hand simply swung into his own chest. It was caught and tied into place. His legs were soon reaching over his head, also tied into place. Soon, a large cock was making its way up Trevor's hole. A frenzied pumping began. His asscheeks were being slapped by gloved hands. A riding crop was striking his chest. Trevor began screaming for help, but his mouth was quickly filled with a Leather gloved hand. The session continued for a long time, until Trevor could feel a geyser of cum shoot up his ass.

The man's voice whispered in his ear, "You will submit to me as my new boy."

It had been a particularly brutal day at work and even though it was a Friday night, Trevor just wanted to shower and crawl into bed. He quickly fell into a deep sleep. The sensation of being carried woke Trevor. Still in that nether world between waking and sleeping, Trevor couldn't realize whether he was in a dream or was someone actually carrying him? He could feel a brawny shoulder underneath his chest.

The clumping of heavy boots descending a flight of steps. The smell of aromatic cigar smoke wafting toward his nostrils. Being thrown against a rough, brick wall. He was standing up – his legs were spreadeagled. His wrists were above his head.

As Trevor struggled toward wakefulness, he viewed the empty basement. "Did someone carry me to the basement?" as he continued to try to wake himself.

As he came to full consciousness, he was spreadeagled on what appeared to be a wooden cross.

"What the FUCK?" Trevor screamed. As his eyes focused, a handsome man in full black Leather stood before him. The Leatherman was puffing on a cigar, furling a bullwhip in his right hand.

"Who the FUCK are you? What are you doing in my...?"

The Leatherman clamped his gloved hand over Trevor's mouth and blew smoke in his face. "That's where you're wrong, pussy boy. This is my house. I'm reclaiming it. You will call me Master Dan." With that, the Leatherman stepped back and expertly landed a single tail whipping on Trevor's right cheek.

Master Dan is once again the Lord of the Manor and shares his house with his slaveboy trevor.

SWEARING

"All right, boy, sit down… I got somethin' to tell you," Daddy said. Daddy's voice was low and soft. The voice scared me – he only used it when he had something bad to tell me. I quickly dropped to my knees and crawled to him. I rested my forehead on his knee.

"Daddy, Sir, what is it?" I questioned. His eyes glistened with tears, an unusual sight for the greatest and strongest man alive.

"Son, I know we've been happy here…"

"NO, Daddy, no, don't get rid of me, don't, Sir, please…," I begged.

His hand stroked the back of my shaven head. "Son, now listen to me… you know damned well it isn't you… now shut up and listen." His hand continued to stroke my head, "And while you're listenin', boy, lick my boots – that'll calm you down."

I dropped to the floor. I spit and licked every inch of his knee-high patrolman boots, hoping that this would express devotion and loyalty toward him.

"It's like this, son... Aaah, this has been our home for some time, you've been my boy for over two years but... Well, son, you know what's been goin' on in the past few months... And what's gonna happen to us both in the next few years. And well, the time's comin', you knew that – for me to relocate... and you as well...I just don't think we're gonna be able to continue this relationship... After all, we're gonna be working in the same city in the same place..."

I stopped the vigorous licking of his boots. "But, Master, you have to keep me as your boy, you can't be serviced by anyone but me, Master... I'm the best boy you've ever had, you've said that all along..."

"That's perfectly true, boy, you have been exceptional, but life is going to be hectic. There are gonna be a lot of pressures, a lot of nosy people... and I just don't know..."

I started crying. "Please, Master, please, don't say this... I couldn't go on without you as my Master... I'm devoted to you. Please, Master..."

"All right, boy." Master said, rubbing the top of my head, "I guess we are a team... We'll work something out."

Two weeks later, Master and I boarded a plane for Washington. I was confident that everything would work out in our personal relationship as Master and Boy. While it was true we would be working together, I also wanted to spend nights at the foot of his bed. Everything in the house had been packed by movers and the house was listed discretely. Master had ordered me to wear a business suit. Over the past two years, he'd made me wear them to all sorts of functions.

As we walked through the terminal, I was miserable.

"Master," I whispered in his ear, "this fuckin' suit feels so horrible..."

"Not now, boy," he responded and he pinched the back of my neck. His signal to me that he would kick the shit out of me when he had the chance if I didn't stop.

I really was tempting fate when I blurted out again, "But, Master, I hate these suits. You've trained me to be your Leatherboy. I prefer my Leather jockstrap and clamps."

"As my Leatherboy, you will obey your Master and wear the suits when I want you to, now, shut the fuck up!"

As we continued through the terminal, we were bombarded with people. I was afraid that we would become separated and so I stuck close to my Master.

Master began talking to several people, introducing me to them as his 'next in command' "Yeah," I thought, "I'm his next in command – whenever there's somebody to push around, it's me!" I pulled at the pants of the tailored suit. "Why in the hell do people wear clothes? They're so uncomfortable."

As we approached the departure gates, we went through the metal detectors, a part of the normal departure routine. Shit, guess who set it off!

"You fuckin' idiot," Master hissed, "what the hell are you wearing?"

"Master, I'm sorry. I've got my titclamps, weights on my balls, and the metal cigar tube up my ass. I was afraid they would get lost in the move… I knew we'd need them when we got to Washington."

"You stupid son-of-a-bitch…" he hissed. His tirade was cut short by the approach of an authoritative man.

"You go right on, Sir," he said apologetically, "Faulty machinery, I'm sure."

The plane awaited our boarding. Soon, we were airborne.

"Sir, can I get you anything?" the flight attendant said to me. I didn't realize she was talking to me, no one had addressed me as 'Sir' in the two years I'd been in Master's possession. He sure as hell didn't call me 'Sir' – 'Dickhead', 'Asswipe', yes. 'Sir', no.

"How about a frothy glass of yellow…"

My Master jabbed me in the ribs, causing me to wince. "He'll have a Perrier."

"Yes, Sir," the flight attendant responded and she left.

"You fuckin' asswipe," he said (See, I told you!) "you were about ready to ask for piss, weren't you? I knew I should have sold you, you fuck-up!"

"I'm sorry, Master, I've been in training for two years now, and it's awfully hard to think as a non-slave..."

"You're still a slave, boy, and don't you forget it." With that he reached down and grabbed my balls through the suit fabric. He gave them a terrible twist.

"Yes, Sir, Master, I'm a sorry piece of shit." I winced as he let go. My balls started throbbing.

"Don't fuck up again, boy, or else it'll be your ass out the emergency door. You'll be landing in a fuckin' cornfield."

Our flight landed two hours later. Throngs of people were waiting for the arrival of the plane, and once again I was afraid to be separated from my Master.

Again, Master stopped to chat with people, some of whom he knew.

"Yes of course, this is Mark Lovejoy..." I heard him say and I nodded uneasily to several of them who glanced in my direction.

"Are you an ex-military man, Mr. Lovejoy? Your hair is so short..."

"Oh, No, Mast... er, Doug likes it that way... it's, ah, disciplined, you might say..." It felt really refreshing to call Master by his first name. "Doug, yeah, Doug, ol' boy," I thought. We were whisked into a waiting limo and soon were barreling through the downtown at an alarming clip.

"Boy, I need you to service me... I've got to release some of this pressure I feel."

The Master pushed my willing head down between his legs. I didn't need a second invitation. I flicked my tongue on the metal zipper once or twice for show. Then, clenching the top of the zipper between my upper and lower jaws, I expertly unzipped it down to the base of the fly. A bulge in Master's pants told me that he was anticipating his worshipful boy's tongue on his dick. But, first, there was the beautiful Leather to work on. Master, even in his most formal business suit, was a tall and dark worshiper of Leather. His dick was encased in a heavy codpiece of studded Leather. Beneath the codpiece, I knew, there would be a heavy Leather cockring encircling his beautiful cock and balls.

I caressed the codpiece with my tongue. I licked each pyramid stud as if they were my Master's exquisite tits.

"Maybe," I thought, "he'll let me play with his tits if I'm really good."

For the moment, Master seemed preoccupied with the speech he was reading. His dick was starting to pulse beneath the heavy, glistening black Leather, but Master was not reacting. I licked and sucked on the Leather, tracing the outline of his big, heavy cock with the very tip of my tongue.

Master absently began stroking my head. "Feels good, boy..." he mumbled as he continued to read the speech. "You'll put the speech down, Doug! if it's the last thing I do..." I thought to myself.

I continued to stroke the man's huge cock through the glistening Leather. The Leather was saturated by my saliva. His cock was pulsing and you could see the mushroom head clearly defined. It was stretching the Leather to its ultimate stretchability.

"Now, Master?"

"Hmmm? Yes, ah, yes, boy... pull the codpiece off."

I artfully pulled the three snaps off with my teeth and dangled the codpiece in my mouth.

"Master?" I said through clenched teeth.

"Yes, boy, drop it on the floor..."

"Shit," I thought, "I certainly like it better when he's beating me – at least I have his undivided attention then... I'm not competing with a fuckin' speech."

I reached in and pulled out his beautiful heavy cock and his big balls through the fabric of his repulsive suit. The Leather cockring was the only saving grace.

Master's dick and balls were breathtaking. I know what you're thinking – every slaveboy says that about his Master's cock and balls, but, in this case, it's really true. "All right, don't take my word for it, fuck you!"

I began my tongued massage of the most beautiful balls and dick on earth. Fuck you, again – it's true.

I traced every single inch of the extended shaft of his dick. I encircled the mushroom head with my tongue, first clockwise, then counter-clockwise. I loved sucking his beautiful nutsac. It was so big – and his nuts hung so low. Slaveboy's dick was throbbing too!

I continued this massage for a good ten minutes.

Master glanced down several times. He seemed lost in watching my tongue for several seconds. I knew that he was beginning to pay less attention to the speech and more attention to the services of his boy.

My tonguing now included a flicking in and out of the piss-slit.

His cock continued to pulse up and down.

Finally, I began to suck the entire cock – gagging the first few times, but finally relaxing my throat enough to take the whole nine inches. It tasted like food of the Gods. At the moment that I first reached the base of Master's shaft, I knew that I was in the presence of a God. My Master. I worshipped and adored him. All these thoughts were circling in my head as I continued to suck his beautiful cock.

Suddenly, Master's hands clamped down on either side of the head, "Yeah, boy, that's what I need – I need your cocksucking mouth to get me off. I need your fuckin' lowly slavemouth to suck the fuckin' bone right out of my dick..." Master was now breathing heavily and moaning softly.

"Come on, boy, do it. Don't sit there, with your tongue stopped. Stop lookin' at me, boy!" I had only glanced up momentarily to see his face. Master was ready for slaveboy to continue, that was for sure. I returned to my duties.

His beautiful manballs were glistening with my spit. I took each one in my mouth and massaged it. Master was beginning to hunker down in the limo seat. He spread his legs so that they were propped up over my shoulders. "That's right, boy, service your Master's nuts... it feels good to have my boy's tongue on them..." He unbuttoned his dress shirt and began rubbing his tits. "Hey," I thought, "that's my job, stop that..."

"Boy, keep your mind on what you're doin'." With that statement, Master pushed my head back down so that I would concentrate on his genitals.

I once again began sucking on his beautiful, extended cock. Master's back arched each time I sucked the cock down to its base.

I sucked harder and harder – once again encircling the cockhead clockwise and then counter-clockwise. I licked droplets of dew from the slit as they formed, knowing it wouldn't take much more to get my Master off. The droplets tasted like the nectar of the Gods. I knew I was in the presence of a really beautiful man, and I was privileged to be his boy. I wanted this to be the best cocksucking of his life. I closed my eyes and sucked harder and harder.

Soon, Mount Vesuvius erupted in my mouth. The man cum lava flowed down my throat in thick, hot cords. I swallowed every drop of my beautiful man's flow.

Finally, I lapped the last drops of his beautiful manworks and leaned back on my haunches.

Master had pulled out a big, black cigar and was stoking it. "Boy, that was the best suckfest you have ever, ever done on me. I'm damned proud of you…" He sighed.

"Thank you, Sir."

"Now turn around and pull down your pants."

"Sir, anything to get out of these wretched pants."

With that, I maneuvered myself around on the limousine floor and lowered those damned pants. My naked ass faced my Master.

"You know, boy, the next few years are gonna be anything but easy," Master said, "and I'm going to need your cooperation and undivided loyalty. Have I got it?" Before I could answer, Master jammed the lighted cigar up my asshole as far as it would go.

"YOWWWW!" I yelled.

The driver of the limousine turned on his intercom and said, "Anything wrong, Sir?" He could not hear any of our goings-on prior to this.

"Nothing, Tony," Master replied.

I spread my asscheeks and rubbed my ass which was burning from the pain. "You know you have my loyalty and love, Master," I replied in a shaky voice.

"Let's see that you maintain that loyalty and love, boy." With that, Master rubbed my ass. He slapped my asscheeks a few times, but these were playful slaps, and soon, the burning of the cigar was a delicious moment in our relationship.

As a result of this unexpected intrusion, my cock had retreated. Soon, Master, had it out, slapping it against the palms of his expert hands. He seemed once again to be preoccupied. He glanced to the seat beside him where the speech lay and read paragraphs of the speech while absently continuing to fondle my dick.

I wanted to shout, "Use it or lose it!" After all, I wanted to jerk off too.

My dick grew in the capable hands of my Master. He even bent over and sucked on it several times, alternating my dick with puffs from his cigar.

Slaveboy's man was a masterful lover and soon I was on the verge of climax. My cock was in Master's mouth when the driver announced over the intercom, "Sir, I'm sorry to interrupt you, but we are almost there."

"Oh, shit," Master replied, my cock still fully engorged in his mouth.

"Ain't no way, Jose, that I'm gonna let you take my cock out of your mouth now..." I thought, as I jammed it further into his mouth.

He muttered something unintelligible, sucked twice, and I shot my load. I shot with such force that I'm surprised it didn't come flying out of his ears! As I looked up, cum was ringing his mouth. He licked his lips hastily.

"Get dressed, you shithead! We're only minutes away from the ceremony. Hurry up! This is it, the moment... Damn you, hurry up." He backhanded me when I fumbled with my disheveled pants.

Somehow, we managed to get everything tucked into place. Master's codpiece once again covering his manworks.

We stepped out of the limousine, greeted with thunderous applause. Cameras flashed, a thousand questions were thrown in our direction. Well-wishers waved flags and flowers over their heads.

Master waved. I followed suit (Oh, I hate that word!).

We walked down a very long carpeted path. The path led to a platform filled with dignitaries. Master led the way, I followed.

Moments later, I watched proudly as my Master, the man with the most beautiful cock and balls in the world, repeated the words, "I, Douglas John McMahon, do solemnly swear that I will uphold the Constitution and Laws of the United States..." My Master had just been sworn in as the 50th President of the United States.

Oh, yeah, and then I was called to the same spot on the platform. I momentarily tugged at those damned pants, before I heard myself repeating after the Supreme Court Justice, "I, Mark Alexander Lovejoy, do solemnly swear…"

Moments later, I had been sworn in as the Vice President of the United States.

THE FLOGGING TREE

It was a hot fucker – the weather, that is. The thermometer read 102 degrees and it felt every bit of it, too. The Leatherman, despite the heat, had on his cod pants, Harley boots, and studded wrist gauntlets, but had discarded his Leather shirt as soon as he walked outside. His alligators bit painfully into his mantits. He relished that feeling. A ballbag pulled deliciously on his cock and balls. He massaged his crotch area with his hands which were encased in a pair of tight, Damascus gloves. He sat on his back porch, smoking a big, black cigar – alternating a draw on the cigar with iced coffee. It was just too fucking hot to work in the yard, even though it desperately needed attention.

As usual, the Leatherman was waiting for a boy. The boy was already 30 minutes overdue. His hide would pay for keeping the Leatherman waiting. The toys of abuse were silently waiting on the porch near the man's booted feet. They were readied for a sojourn in the woods with the boy. The cool interior of the woods – with a boy tied tightly to a tree. Things would certainly heat up even more when, and if, the boy showed up.

The boy was a Philadelphia sub. He had been persistent in his attempts to secure an 'audience' with the Leatherman.

"I want to be worked over by a Leatherman – a man from the Old Guard. No mercy on my ass." the boy had written.

"Not to worry, boy, no mercy is shown from this LeatherMaster," the Leatherman had replied.

Finally, one hour, fifteen minutes late, the boy arrived.

The Leatherman regarded the boy silently through his mirrored sunglasses.

The boy slowly emerged from his car, wearing ass-tight chaps, jeans, a white tee shirt, and harness boots. The boy got extra points – he was wearing his Damascus gloves.

The boy climbed the steps and knelt before the Leatherman, head bowed, hands behind his back.

"You're late, boy."

"My apologies, Sir. A traffic accident tied up traffic, Sir. I left a message on your answering machine, Sir."

The Leatherman accepted the boy's apology, but indicated that there would be added punishment.

The boy silently accepted the pronouncement.

"Lick my boots, boy."

The boy began tonguing the Leatherman's dirty boots and kept on task, doing a decent job. The Leatherman swatted him occasionally, just to remind him who was Boss.

Finally, the Leatherman indicated that the boy had done a good job. He drew the boy's mouth toward his own and gave the boy a long, tongued kiss.

"Thank you, Sir."

"Time for a session, boy. Take off the jeans and tee shirt. Chaps & boots back on."

The boy stripped, revealing a handsome cock and balls. He presented himself for inspection.

The Leatherman squeezed the boy's cock and balls with one hand. The other hand reached in the toy bag and extracted a two pound ballbag. He placed it at the base of the boy's privates. The Leatherman brought out a pair of clamps and attached them to the boy's nipples. The boy flinched but said nothing.

"Follow me, boy," the Leatherman indicated that the boy should pick up the toy bag as he marched across his property. He led the boy down a bank to a shallow creek into a dense woods. The boy hesitated as they ascended the bank into the woods for which he received a slap across the left cheek.

"Boy, follow me. Don't lag." The Leatherman continued to lead the way, marching confidently to his favored flogging spot. A substantial tree. More than one boy had been tied to it and worked over.

The boy was ordered to face the tree. The Leatherman made certain that the boy's cock was pressed against the rough tree bark. He pulled on the ballbag so that it hung down between the boy's legs. He kicked the boy's legs apart. With that, he placed wrist restraints on the boy's wrists, securing them with bondage rope. The boy was now hugging the tree. A Leather hood was extracted from the bag and tightly laced over the boy's head. The hood's eyeholes were covered with a snap-on mask and a snap-on plug was inserted in the boy's mouth.

"Not quite finished, boy," the Leatherman said as he encircled the boy's booted feet with restraints. He then placed a spacer bar between them, keeping the legs spread.

Finally, bondage rope trussed the boy's chest closely to the tree. The boy was now fully the Leatherman's captive.

"Now, we're ready," he flatly stated and the protracted session of floggings began. He used his heaviest flogger. The boy wrenched his body in the tight confines of the restraints. The flogger caught his shoulder blades, upper back and asscheeks with its biting tails. The boy's head twisted from side to side, eventually coming to rest against the tree, bowed in acceptance and submission.

Both man and boy broke into a sweat, sweat dripping down their backs. The Leatherman felt invigorated as he continued to lay on the lashes. It was purely sexual for him as his cock hardened in his Leather pouch. The boy was his property, his slave boy, his piece of boymeat. And there was no one around to stop him from this activity.

As he continued to flog, he occasionally reached around to increase the pressure on the boy's nipclamps, or pull on the ballbag, stretching the boy's nutsac. The boy's cock was hardened and throbbing against the tree.

After a prolonged flogging, the Leatherman placed the flogger on the D ring of his pants. He pulled out his butt paddle – a mean muthafucker by any standard.

The boy's ass received fifty hard whacks with the paddle with no stops. The boy flinched and his body attempted to avoid the paddlings by listing from side to side, but to no avail. The butt paddle always found its target.

Halfway through the paddlings, the Leatherman pulled out his bonehard rod. It was readied for action with a massaging of the Leatherman's free hand. The boy's ass was blood red as Number 50 completed the rotation.

The boy slumped against the tree, but the man forcibly yanked the boy's body to an upright position. The Leatherman fingered the boy's hole, spit on his own cock, and jammed his manrod as far as it would go. The boy's muffled screams could be heard through the Leather hood as the man's cock invaded the boy's tight hole.

The Leatherman reached around and pulled on the boy's aching nips. His screams could be heard, but ignored. It only made the Leatherman hornier. He pulled and twisted on them as his cock thrust in and out of the boy's ravaged ass.

"Take it, boy. Take your man's seed up your fuckhole," the Leatherman growled. His Leathered body slammed into the boy's body as the cockpumping became even more frenzied.

"Fuck, it feels so good," the Leatherman snorted as sweat dripped from the brim of his Muir cap and landed on the shoulders and back of the boy. The boy's arms flexed and his hands gripped the tree as hard as he could. He wrestled with the wrist restraints, but nothing would loosen them, nor would anything relieve the pain of the Leatherman's fucktool up his ass.

The boy was breathing heavily and sweating profusely. His Master's sweat and his own sweat created a lubricated layer between the boy's back and the man's muscular chest.

The Leatherman continued to pump for some time, not wanting to climax. It just felt too damned good.

The boy's asscheeks closed around the Leatherman's cock and his cock reacted. A load of cum shot up the boy's ass with a mighty heave.

"FUCK!" screamed the Leatherman and even the boy's screams were audible as his ass accepted the manjuice up his battered hole.

The Leatherman and boy stood silently for a long time, as the Master continued to glide his cock in and out of the receptacle.

Finally, he withdrew. He unmanacled the boy. The boy's cock was pulsating. The ballbag hung in place on the boy's swollen balls.

Restraining the boy with his back to the tree, the Leatherman pulled a small cockteaser off of his D ring.

He lightly flogged the boy's cock. Pre-cum appeared in the piss slit.

The Leatherman slammed his body into the boy.

His Leathered hand gripped the cock and balls in a vicelike grip.

"I want to see you cum, boy."

It didn't take any prompting as the boy's cock shot a stream of cum a good distance. Some landed on the Master's gloves.

The Leatherman slapped the boy across the cheek and forcefed the boy with his gloved fingers.

"Lick it clean, boy. Lick your slavecum off my gloves."

The boy was quick in obeying his Master's orders.

The Leatherman released the boy from his restraints. The boy dropped to the ground.

The Leatherman planted his right boot in the middle of the boy's sweaty chest.

"Lick my boot, boy. You're not done."

When the boy had serviced the right boot, the left boot was firmly planted on the boy's chest which was covered in sweat and grime.

The boy's tongued the second boot and seemed to revive from the servicing.

"Up, boy," the Leatherman ordered and pressed the boy's mouth against his clamped nips.

"Suck on my nips, boy. Pull on the chain with your teeth."

The boy did this reluctantly, but the Leatherman's hand forced the boy's head firmly against his chest.

"Harder, boy."

The titpain was delicious. The Leatherman's back arched to receive the pleasure.

All the time, the man was holding the two cocks side by side. Both had revived and with the feel of the Leather glove, both had once again hardened.

It took some time for the cockrubbings to maximize the hardness of both cocks, but eventually both had bones in them again.

Both Master and slave were breathing heavily. Their bellies heaving against one another.

The Leatherman increased the frequency of rubbing until the boy's cock could not hold it in any longer. He shot against the Leather of the man's pants. He was ordered to kneel with his cock still dripping and to take his Master's cock in his mouth.

The Leatherman thrust his hardened rod further and further into the boy's mouth until his cock reached a second climax. The boy lapped up every drop and then cleaned off the cum on his LeatherMaster's pants.

"All right, boy, that was a good session. We will adjourn to the dungeon." He led the boy back across the creek and into the dungeon. He was tied to a St. Andrew's Cross and the flogging continued. After all, he had to be disciplined for being late.

THE FORTUNATE ACCIDENT

It was a beautiful day and I had a rare day off from work. "Twist my arm," I thought, "let's take the Harley out for a spin." I suited up in my cycle jacket, knee-high Dehners, chaps over my old comfortable jeans, and of course, my tight, black Damascus gloves. Just for good measure, I put on my cockring, heavy Leather harness, and studded armbands. There wasn't a cloud in the sky as I zipped out of my driveway onto the country road in front of my house. Pretty soon, I was traveling country roads out into the deep country, passing farmland, cows in the pasture, and Amish farmers plowing their fields with mules and hand-drawn plows.

I should have looked over my shoulder because I had failed to notice one black cloud, one ominously black cloud, as I continued to cycle further away from home.

Seemingly without warning, a clap of thunder was followed by a torrential downpour of rain. Before I could even get my cycle off to the side of the road, I was broadsided by a strong gust of wind and rain and my Harley skidded off the side of the road. I had the sensation of impact before I lost consciousness.

I woke briefly to realize that I was being gently placed on a stretcher. My left leg was gingerly being placed back into a normal position as I once again lost consciousness.

I woke briefly to realize that I was in a hospital bed, wearing one of those unmanly hospital robes before I lapsed into sleep. I slept and woke, slept and woke. My brain rationalized that I must be on some sort of painkiller, was it morphine they give you, before I lapsed into sleep once again.

I guess it had been several days when I finally became more aware of my surroundings. I had the sensation that someone was sponging my back. Now, I am a loner and I enjoy my privacy unless I give permission for a boy to share my 'space', and it seemed to me that it was being invaded.

"Who?" was all I could manage to say and that was with difficulty. My speech was slurred and the person probably just thought I was speaking gibberish.

"I'm Tony... just relax... you may not realize it but you were in a pretty serious accident..." said a man's voice. Through my blurred vision, I noticed that my left leg was immobilized in a cast and was suspended from a pulley system. That's all I remember before falling asleep once again.

As the days passed (I assume they were days, I lost track of time), Tony would come to my room to give me my sponge bath. My eyes were refocusing and each time I garnered a few more details for my memory bank. He was handsome. He had black curly hair, big brown eyes, and muscular arms.

Several times I tried to sit up and I was pushed back into place.

"Now just relax, Sir." Tony said.

As I improved, I looked forward to Tony's daily visits. No one from work had bothered to come see me (as far as I knew). I assume the hospital had called and told them I wouldn't be returning for an extended period of time. And they didn't even bother to send me a fucking card… not one damned card was anywhere to be seen.

"Well, good morning, handsome," Tony said as he entered the room. On this occasion, I noticed that he was wearing a vee-necked scrub shirt, revealing a very hairy chest with two mounds of titflesh. "Damn, he's a cute little fucker," I thought, "I'd tie him up in my playroom and have clamps on those in no time at all."

"You are feeling better, aren't you?" as he playfully tweaked the mound in my hospital gown. He lifted it and intoned the word "Mercy!" before placing it back in place and grinning.

It was then that a pain shot through my cock like nothing I had ever felt before.

"Sir, try not to get aroused. You have a catheter in you… we're helping you pee…"

I was always proud of my cock, but wasn't anxious to share it with everybody. However, Tony was cute and I must have been getting better because there was a definite sexual tingle simply from viewing this young man. That tingle, of course, translated into an aroused cock. At this point, not a good fucking thing.

As Tony prepared the bath water and sponge, I couldn't help but notice his cute asscheeks, filling out his green scrubs rather nicely.

I tried to quell my sexual urges because it hurt so damned much, and having a tube stuck up your pisshole sure as hell did not help matters.

As he washed my chest and arms, I noted a tenting in the front of his scrubs.

I playfully reached for his hidden cock, but a pain shot through my arm. I looked with horror at the number of bruises and swelling on it.

"Now, Sir, just relax…" as he repositioned my arm by my side. "You're lucky you didn't break anything else, but you did a pretty good number on yourself as it is. Your leg is going to require at least another surgery and therapy."

Shit, this was bad news. "Whaaatt... about my cycle?" I anxiously asked.

"It took the brunt of the accident, Sir. You're lucky in that respect. It skidded into a tree. Your leg was crushed underneath it. But, if you had gone head first, well, we wouldn't be talking. See, it could have been worse."

Shit, again. I loved that cycle. It was an essential part of me – it was part of my identity as a Leatherman. As a cycleman. Shit. I was feeling pretty sorry for myself.

"We're just glad that you survived – we need more handsome men like you around, for us boys... to teach us the ropes." With that, Tony caressed my forehead, leaned down, and kissed my cheek. I had plenty of time to mull over all that he said that afternoon.

The next day, Tony returned to bathe me. He confessed that he had seen my profile on a Leather website and recognized me.

"I was too intimidated to message you, Sir, but you are part of my jerk-off fantasies..." With that he lowered his eyes and continued to the task at hand.

"Come here, son." Tony laid down the sponge and I motioned for him to lean down. I kissed him, my tongue exploring his mouth.

"Thank you, son. You are an excellent son, and any Leatherman would be proud to have you as his boy."

"Thank you, Sir."

As I continued to improve, I really looked forward to Tony's visits.

On this particular morning, I was feeling much better. Itching to get out of bed. Itching to have my soft, comfortable Leathers caressing me.

"Tony, what happened to my Leathers and, ur, my accessories?"

"Relax, Daddy," Tony replied, "they are hanging in the closet, waiting for your return to them… However, Sir…" With that he hesitated.

"What, son?"

"They had to cut your boot off your foot."

Shit, again. Not my Dehners.

He held up the mangled remains of my boot. My chaps and jacket were neatly hung over hangers, as was my harness. The chaps had a big tear in the knee and the jacket was pitted from road rash.

"Damn," I exclaimed.

"Don't worry about it, handsome. Once you get back on your feet – you'll be back in them, as masculine as ever. Therapy, by the way, starts tomorrow." With that he leaned down and kissed me.

With difficulty, they got me out of bed the next morning and I began the prescribed therapy to regain strength in my leg which was now pieced together. It ached in more places than I can count. But, after all, I am a Leatherman and can endure pain. That isn't to say that I wasn't ready to give up on more than one occasion when shooting pains went through every part of my leg.

That first day of therapy I was returned to the hospital bed. I was soaked in sweat and looked forward to my sponge bath.

A bull nurse charged into the room with the basin, sponge and fresh catheter tubing. Talk about a female Nazi. Guess she hated men because she sure as hell did not have the bedside manner that Tony had. She twisted and pulled on my cock until I thought it would pull off in her hands.

It intensified my yearnings for that cute boy.

"Where's Tony?" I demanded.

"Oh, his rotation on this floor is through… I'll be taking care of you for the next week…"

"Well," I rationalized in my mind, "I won't have to worry about getting a hard-on for awhile."

The therapy continued and I was feeling steadier on my feet. I had a decided limp but realized, by and by, that I was fortunate not to have been banged up any more than I was.

Finally, I was allowed a man's privilege of taking a piss – the catheter was removed.

The next day Tony showed up with a shit-eating grin on his face.

"I hear Daddy can hold his cock by himself. Donna doesn't have to do it for you any more."

"You fucker…" I said, but smiled at him.

He closed the private room door. He leaned over and lifted my hospital gown. My cock had swollen from seeing the handsome boy.

He kneeled beside the bed and tenderly placed my cock in his mouth. He not only knew how to give a man a sponge bath, but a tongue-bath as well. It felt so good. My cock had not been juiced up by a boy since the accident, of course, and so, it felt doubly good. My cock swelled to its old proportions. The boy soaked my whole pole, occasionally catching my balls with that fantastic tongue.

I drifted back to the good old days before the accident. I imagined I was in full Leather, relaxing in my Leather chair, dragging on a cigar.

A dutiful boy fulfilling his Daddy's needs.

He came up for air, but with my injured arm, I managed to push his head back down.

"Continue sucking, boy, until Daddy shoots…," I ordered. I knew it wouldn't take long.

"Yes, Daddy," he answered before resuming his duties.

I soon shot a load, worthy of my former days. Tony licked the residue from his lips, got up off his knees, leaned over and kissed me on the forehead.

"Rest well, Daddy," he said, as he exited the room.

Finally, after an excruciatingly long time, I was released from the hospital. My old Leatherbuddy Mike came to pick me up – in his truck, by the way. I wasn't anxious to be on a cycle just yet. He had picked up jeans, well-worn work boots, and a tee shirt for me to wear home. I insisted on putting on my damaged chaps and my cycle jacket to leave the hospital.

It was so good to be home. I leafed through the pile of mail, bills from the hospital, and my suspension notice and subsequent termination notice from work. "Failure to report to work." Fuck, nobody had bothered to call them.

On the second day at home, in the late afternoon, the doorbell sounded. I hobbled to the door.

When I opened it, there was Tony, grinning from ear to ear. "Hello, Sir," as he walked in and knelt at my feet. He wore a tight pair of Leather shorts, a bar vest, and boots.

"I have come to serve you."

Looks like the Leather gods were looking out for me after all, they had sent me a guardian angel.

With no pain felt, my cock rose in my pants and I escorted him upstairs to our bedroom.

*This story originally appeared in
The Flagship, Winter 2007 (Issue 77).*

APPROPRIATE GIFTS FOR A LEATHERMAN

The Leatherdaddy had not gone to bed until 3:30 AM after a very strenuous day – the celebration of his fiftieth birthday. Since he figured it was his day, he could do anything he wanted. He had slept in and then enjoyed his morning coffee on the back porch in his softest, favorite Leathers. He prearranged to have his favorite boy carl there for the afternoon and they spent it with the boy between Daddy's legs giving the Daddy a very prolonged suck massage of the Daddy's cock. It was exhilarating and the Daddy and the boy had then tumbled around in the Daddy's king-sized bed on Leather sheets. He had given the boy off the day in terms of being flogged or tied up. The boy had prepared the Daddy's favorite meal and they had eaten by candlelight. After the meal, Daddy lighted his favorite cigar while the boy knelt nearby.

At about eight PM, a knock sounded on the back door. When the boy answered the door, he was greeted by a dozen of the Leatherman's closest Leather friends. They roared into the house with bottles of booze, boxes of cigars, and two very attractive slaves. The boyslaves were both big and muscular, with shaved heads. Their clothing was quickly shed to reveal their handsome, naked bodies. Fucking and sucking continued until the wee hours of the morning when the Daddy finally indicated that it was time to call it a night. After all, he was fifty and a day! The Leathermen shuffled the guys out the door. The Leatherdaddy even sent his boy home.

He climbed up the steps wearily and discarded his boots on the landing. He fell into bed exhausted, but woke up around five thirty. A cock full of piss made him reluctantly get out of bed and stumble to the bathroom. As he groggily shuffled to the bathroom, he stubbed his toe into something solid. "Shit," he thought, "I must have left my boots there…" He continued his journey, not bothering to turn on the light. He massaged his dick before aiming for the toilet bowl. He did not hear the usual stream of piss hitting the sides of the bowl. "Odd," he momentarily thought, but he was still half asleep. He continued to relieve himself. When he reached over to flush, his hand encountered the head of someone. That woke Daddy up!

"Sir, thank you for the piss. I am honored to receive it from such a handsome man."

"Whaa…" the Daddy fumbled to recover his language skills.

He flicked the light on and there sitting obediently was one of the boyslaves. His mouth and chest drenched in manpiss. The boy was wiping it off with his fingers and licking it. The boy fell silent.

"Well, um, thank you, boy – I didn't know you were still here…"

"Yes, Sir, we are your birthday gifts for the weekend from your Leather friends."

"We? There's more?"

Kneeling in the hallway, head lowered and hands behind his back was the other boyslave. The solid object the man had stumbled over.

"Sir, it is an honor to serve you – we are here to do whatever you wish…" the second boyslave said.

"Right, now, boys, Daddy needs more sleep..." and he stumbled back into bed. When he woke later that morning, he thought, "It must have been a dream..." but as he looked toward the bedroom door there were two boyslaves, shaved heads, naked except for boots and socks, arms behind their backs. They were kneeling at his bedside.

"Okay, boys, you're a dream, but it's a real dream." His lecherous mind leaped into action.

The boys made coffee and breakfast and served the Daddy on the backporch.

The sun rose in the sky, producing a picture-perfect day and the Daddy meant to take full advantage of his presents.

It was nearing noon when he ordered the boys to the yard. They were naked except for their boots and socks. He spread an Army blanket on the grassy backyard.

"Face down, side by side, on the blanket, boys." The boys quickly complied.

Their asses were irresistible, just begging to be worked over by a Leatherman.

The Daddy had dressed in chaps, a cockring, boots, gloves, and a harness. He retrieved his toys from the toolshed.

At first, he paddled the boys' asses slowly, increasing the intensity with each strike. The boys never flinched, never moaned. In fact, their asses arched upward to receive each paddling. They took it like the submissives they were.

He rubbed the reddened asses with his soft gloves and then proceeded to flog the boy's handsome backs. Again, they never flinched as the Leather strips bit into their naked backs.

The Daddy knelt, placing each of his knees between the two pair of legs. He once again rubbed each boy's ass before fingering their boyholes with his gloved hands.

A bottle of lube pulled from his toolbag lubricated each gloved hand. He inserted first his thumb and then the rest of his fingers into each of the boys' willing holes. The warm summer day was an aphrodisiac, making him hornier. As he explored the boys' holes, he broke into a healthy mansweat. It dripped from his forehead and chest onto the backs of the boys, mixing with their own sweat. They both lay silently, but each had a smile on his face. Their newly-found Leatherdaddy was an excellent fister. The Daddy's cock, already hard, was arching skyward, worshipping the sun.

His mansweat ran down his back onto his asscheeks and down the legs of his meaty thighs.

After a prolonged session of fistfucking, the man withdrew his gloved hands. The boys raised their heads, questioning the decision.

"Relax, boys, more to come…"

He reached into his toolbag and pulled out two dildos. Greased up, a dildo was inserted into each butt of the boys.

The Daddy knelt in front of the first boy, guiding his mancock into the boy's mouth. The boy raised himself up enough to get Daddy's cock into his mouth and vacuumed the man's bone until the Daddy couldn't hold it any longer.

He gripped the boy's jaw and pushed his cock into the boy's mouth until it would go no further. He came very quickly down the willing boy's throat.

The second boy lay patiently. "On your knees, boy," the Leatherman ordered as he pulled his cock out of the first boy's mouth.

"Lick it, boy," the Leatherman ordered as he stood up.

Eye level with the delicious meat, the boy did not need a second moment to reconsider before he was chowing down on the cum-covered cock.

It was usual for the man to take a piss after jacking off and so the second boy was treated to a stream of piss down his throat. He apparently relished it because he was gulping greedily during the episode.

When finished, the man ordered the other boy on his knees. Until then, he was laying quietly, relishing the taste of the Daddy's cum. The boy was quick to comply, however.

With that the Daddy pressed the boys' heads into his chest and ordered each of them to service his manly nips. Both boys must have had considerable experience with this service too, because they were soon sucking and tonguing his nip rings.

The Daddy was fondling his cock which was already hard again. When the Daddy was ready to come again, he reversed the order of performance. Like the well-trained and obedient boys they were, the dildos remained in the boys' holes until the Daddy removed them. He then led the boys to the back porch where they once again assumed submissive positions. Heads bowed, kneeling in front of him, hands behind their backs.

He ordered one to fetch him a cigar while the other was ordered to position himself on all fours, serving as a footstool. The first boy returned, having punched his Daddy's cigar and with the match ready to strike. The boy returned to a kneeling position in front of the Leatherman.

The Daddy absently fondled his dick. The boys watched his every move, never making eye contact, of course. They were apparently eager to taste his manmeat once again. The Leatherman played with his cock and balls and enjoyed the cigar for a few minutes while planning his next activity.

When ready, the Daddy pulled his flogger off the D ring of his chaps and began flogging each boy in turn. They seemed to relish it, like complacent dogs who continue to wag their tails even after being beaten. The man reached down and pulled the Footstool's tits. Pretty soon, the tits were in the vicelike grip of the Leatherman's tight, black Damascus gloves. The boy momentarily flinched. In short order, the man's nipclamps were biting into the boy's nips.

"Boy, go get me my toolbag," the Daddy said to the other boy.

The boy hastily retrieved it and presented it to him with bowed head.

A second pair of nipclamps were placed on Retriever's nips.

Halfway through his cigar, the Daddy ordered his boys to "Present your asses for inspection." The boys complied to the Leatherman's command. He reached between their legs and grabbed their cock and balls. He squeezed tightly. Tight black Leather gloves encircling the boys' privates were a 'hardening' agent for the boys' cocks, however, the Leatherdaddy warned them. "Don't you cum, boys!" Their mutual faces contorted as they tried hard not to jack off with their masculine Leatherman's gloved hands squeezing and manipulating their cocks. They were good boys and held it in.

He ordered them into the toolshed. Footstool was placed spreadeagle on the workover table and Retriever on a St. Andrew's cross.

Like a whirling dervish, the Daddy's flogger lashed the boy on the table and a second flick of the flogger sent a licking across the boy's chest on the cross. The lashings continued for a good twenty minutes until he turned over both boys and repeated the action on their asses and back. Since there was more territory to cover, this lashing was a longer session – until both boys were covered in reddened lash marks over most of their respective bodies.

"I'm not through with you yet, boys..." the Daddy promised. The boys both beamed, but then quickly lost their smiles as the serious whipping began.

As he continued the lashings, the Leatherman's cock was fully extended and he knew he had to relieve himself of more of his manseed. He crawled on top of the naked boy on the workover table. The Leatherman's nearly naked, sweaty body fit perfectly into the curvature of the boy's back and his handsome ass. The man began sliding up and down, holding on to the boy's extended arms, which were elevated above the boy's body, firmly held in place by the wrist restraints and chains. The boy apparently relished the feeling, responding to the stimulation. The boy's asscheeks expanded and contracted and his shoulder muscles were flexing. The Leatherman was quick to stick his dick between the asscheeks as they flexed. The boy's head reared back as he felt the Daddy's cock between his asscheeks. It was the only time the boy had spoken to the Leatherman during sessions.

"Please, Sir, fuck me. Fuck me with your big cock. I want to feel your seed." The boy flexed his ass muscles so that the Leatherman's cock was held between the boy's asscheeks.

The Daddy increased the sliding motion, getting harder and harder.

The boy moaned as the Daddy's breathing became more labored.

The Daddy was rubbing the boy's back and ribcage with his gloved hands. He continued to rub his masculine body against the boy's back, reaching underneath to squeeze the boy's nips, cock and balls. The man's cock was getting harder inside the boy's butt as his balls slapped against the boy's asscheeks.

Within minutes, the man shot a load of cum which spilled out onto the table.

"Fuck, yeah, I'm gonna be fifty again next year," the Leatherman thought as he crawled off of the boy and eyed the other slaveboy's naked ass.

ABOUT THE AUTHOR

G.W. Leatherman Parks has been a Leatherman for over thirty years. He is a proud member of the Leather Archives and Museum in Chicago and writes frequently for FLAGSHIP, the newsletter of Fits Like a Glove. He has also been published in *Drummer and Cuir: For LeatherMen by LeatherMen.* He is a collector of vintage Leather, Leather artwork and photography.

This is G.W. Leatherman Parks' fourth book. His first book *Leatherdaddy,* second book *Leather Nazis,* and third book *A Harvest of G.O.L.D.: Leather Bikers on the Prowl* are available from Amazon.com, TheNazcaPlainsCorp.com or your local bookstore.

LEATHERDADDY

Erotic Literature by the Black Leather Gloved Hands of

G.W. LEATHERMAN PARKS

A BONER BOOK

Leather Nazis

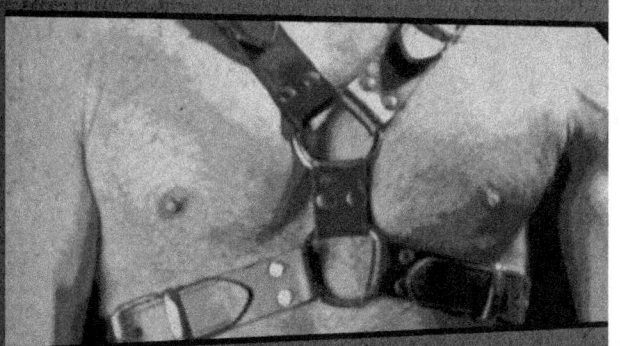

Erotic Literature by
the Black Leather Gloved Hands of

G.W. Leatherman Parks

A Boner Book

PARKS

A HARVEST OF G.O.L.D.

A HARVEST OF G.O.L.D.
LEATHER BIKERS ON THE PROWL

G.W. LEATHERMAN PARKS

A
BONER
BOOK